W9-AHY-825

Suddenly, something green flashed in the night sky.

"Hey! What was that?" Wishbone asked.

The dog looked at Joe and Sam. The kids had sat up and were pointing at the sky.

"It was over there!" Joe said excitedly.

A moment later, David came running from next door. "Did you see what just happened?" he asked.

"I think so," said Sam.

"Wow!" said Joe, his eyes wide. "There it is again!"

Wishbone followed the direction in which Joe pointed. The dog saw it a second time—a flash of something green in the night sky. And this time, it remained exactly in one spot, as if daring them to believe in it.

Then the green glow began to grow dim. It looked as if it were evaporating. It kept on moving, getting dimmer and dimmer, until it had finally disappeared.

Suddenly, a distant explosion rocked the stillness of the night. Wishbone and his friends jumped.

"Sounded like a crash," Joe said.

"A big crash," David remarked.

Books in the
WISHBONE™ Mysteries series:

Books in the WISHBONE
SUPER Mysteries series:

*coming soon

WISHBONE Mysteries

THE SIRIAN CONSPIRACY

by Michael Jan Friedman and Paul Kupperberg

WISHBONE™ created by Rick Duffield

Big Red Chair Books™, *A Division of* **Lyrick Publishing**™

If you purchased this book without a cover, you should be aware that this book is stolen property. It was reported as "unsold and destroyed" to the publisher, and neither the authors nor the publisher have received any payment for this "stripped book."

This book is a work of fiction. The characters, incidents, and dialogues are products of the authors' imagination and are not to be construed as real. Any resemblance to actual events or persons, living or dead, is entirely coincidental.

Big Red Chair Books™, *A Division of Lyrick Publishing*™
300 E. Bethany Drive, Allen, Texas 75002

©1999 Big Feats! Entertainment

All rights reserved. No part of this book may be used or reproduced in any manner whatsoever without written permission of the publisher, except in the case of brief quotations embodied in critical articles and reviews. For information address **Lyrick Publishing**™, 300 E. Bethany Drive, Allen, Texas 75002

Edited by Kevin Ryan

Copy edited by Jonathon Brodman

Continuity editing by Grace Gantt

Cover concept and design by Lyle Miller

Interior illustrations by Kathryn Yingling

Wishbone photograph by Carol Kaelson

Library of Congress Catalog Card Number: 98-89361

ISBN: 1-57064-588-4

First printing: June 1999

10 9 8 7 6 5 4 3 2 1

WISHBONE, the **Wishbone** portrait, and the Big Feats! Entertainment logo are trademarks and service marks of Big Feats! Entertainment. **Big Red Chair Books** and **Lyrick Publishing** are trademarks and service marks of Lyrick Studios, Inc. **Big Red Chair Books** is a Reg. U.S. Pat. & Tm. Off.

Printed in the United States of America

*For Hunter, Mugsy, Dylan,
Cosmo, and Bailey*
—Mike Friedman

For Max
—Paul Kupperberg

FROM THE BIG RED CHAIR . . .

Oh . . . hi! Wishbone here. You caught me right in the middle of some of my favorite things—books. Let me welcome you to the WISHBONE Mysteries. In each story, I help my human friends solve a puzzling mystery. In *THE SIRIAN CONSPIRACY*, my friends and I see a green, glowing object shoot through the black sky over Oakdale. When we investigate this UFO, Sam, David, Joe, and I uncover top-secret information and a suspicious cover-up.

The story takes place in the summer, during the same period as the events that you'll see in the second season of my **WISHBONE®** television show. In this story, Joe is fifteen, and he and his friends are about to enter the ninth grade. Like me, they are always ready for adventure . . . and a good mystery.

You're in for a real treat, so pull up a chair, grab a snack, and sink your teeth into *THE SIRIAN CONSPIRACY!*

Chapter One

"Well, this is rather pleasant," Wishbone said.

The little white-with-brown-and-black-spots Jack Russell terrier was lying comfortably on the lawn in front of the house where he lived.

It was a beautiful, warm, summer Saturday night in Oakdale. The grass felt smooth and cool against Wishbone's side, and it smelled even better.

Wishbone was with his best friend, Joe Talbot, and one of Joe's best pals, Samantha Kepler. The kids were lying on their backs, looking up at the stars that were splattered like white paint drops against the black night sky.

All they had to do for the rest of the night was . . . well, nothing. Nothing at all.

Boy, thought Wishbone, *this is almost as good as a run through the park or a hard game of fetch with Joe . . . or an afternoon session spent digging in the sweet-smelling earth of Wanda's flower beds.*

It was every dog's dream night. Every kid's, too.

"This is great," Joe said, totally content. He was a handsome boy with brown hair and dark eyes.

"Yeah," said Samantha, whose nickname was Sam. Her hazel eyes sparkled and her long blond hair fanned out around her head.

Suddenly, something green flashed in the sky. Wishbone jumped up with a quick, sharp bark when he caught sight of it.

"Hey!" he said. "What was that?"

He looked at Joe and Sam. The kids had sat up and were pointing at the sky.

"It was over there!" Joe said excitedly.

Sam didn't say anything, but her mouth was hanging wide open.

A moment later, David Barnes came running from next door. David, a curious-minded boy who was a whiz at science, was Joe's other best human pal.

"Did you just see what happened?" David asked, barely able to contain himself.

"I think so," said Sam. "It flashed and was gone so quickly, I wouldn't have been sure—except Joe said he saw it, too."

"Wow!" said Joe, his eyes as wide as a pair of dog dishes. "There it is again!"

Wishbone followed the direction in which Joe pointed. The dog saw it a second time—a flash of something green in the night sky. And this time, it remained exactly in one spot, as if daring them to believe in it.

To the terrier, the glowing object looked to be about the size of a baseball. However, he had no way of knowing just how high up in the sky it was. For all he knew, it might have been huge, high up and just barely visible to them on the ground.

Then the glow shot through the black sky like an

airplane. Unfortunately, the terrier had no way to tell how fast it was moving.

"It's just like the last time!" said David.

Wishbone looked at the boy and saw that his dark brown eyes were wide open, locked on the mysterious green object. The terrier felt a shiver of excitement. His tail wagged wildly.

"That's right," Wishbone said. "Just like the last time!"

David swallowed hard as he stared at the unidentified flying object. His heart pounded with a combination of excitement and fear.

Then he forced himself to think about the UFO the way a scientist would, logically and without emotion. He had wanted another chance to study the mysterious object that he and his friends had sighted the year before. Now he had gotten that chance, and he had to make the most of it.

By squinting, David could make out the center of the glow, where the green light was the brightest. It appeared to be a ball of some sort, but it was hard to be sure. Try as he might, David was unable to tell if the object was solid, like a balloon, or if it was made of some sort of gas. It just rolled steadily and swiftly from one side of the night sky to the other.

David heard Wishbone let out a growl, and he glanced at the terrier. Wishbone's back had stiffened, and he had bared his teeth. He looked as if he were defending the kids from the mysterious intruder.

As though in response to Wishbone's behavior, the

green glow began to grow dim. It looked as if it were evaporating.

"It's disappearing," Joe whispered.

Whatever was happening to the glow didn't seem to stop it from rolling through the sky. It kept on moving, getting dimmer and dimmer, until it had finally disappeared.

David kept staring up at the sky. So did his friends. All they saw now was stars—bright, twinkling lights from far, far away. Perfectly normal, David thought. But he couldn't stop staring.

"That was amazing!" Joe exclaimed.

"You said it!" Sam agreed breathlessly.

"But what was it?" David muttered.

"Remember the last time we saw the green glow?" Joe asked. "Everybody denied that it could be an alien spaceship."

David shrugged. "Well, they were right. It wasn't a spaceship. You and I proved that, Joe. It was a hoax, a practical joke. Besides, there's never been one tiny bit of proof that aliens exist, much less that they've ever visited Earth."

"They could just be really careful about being spotted," Joe said matter-of-factly.

"Sure," said Sam. "They could be sneaking around in their flying saucers so we don't catch them."

"Come on!" David said. "Think of the satellites that orbit Earth, collecting data on weather patterns and watching space for things like meteors and comets. And there's hardly a patch of sky in the world that isn't covered by radar used for military or civilian aviation. If even the smallest number of all those reports about aliens was true, there would be solid proof of their existence."

"But we never got an explanation for the green glow we saw last year," Joe pointed out. "And now that—"

Suddenly, a distant explosion rocked the stillness of the night. David jumped, startled. His first thought was that the UFO had launched an attack and that the aliens were firing on the kids with their laser beams!

He looked around in alarm, but he didn't see anything. Then he realized that the sound had come from far away.

David laughed a little nervously. He had let his imagination get the best of him. There weren't any aliens or laser beams. He had just been spooked by the green glow.

At least that was what he told himself.

But . . . if the explosion hadn't come from an alien ship, David asked himself, where *had* it come from?

"Sounded like a crash," Joe said.

"A big crash," David remarked.

"And it came maybe five seconds after the glow disappeared from view," Sam added.

David frowned as he thought about it. "Do you think—?" he started to ask. Suddenly, he was interrupted by the excited chatter of voices all around him.

Drawn by the sound of the distant explosion, people were coming out of their houses on Forest Lane, the street on which Joe and David lived. David's parents, Ruth and Nathan Barnes, were the first ones out their door, their faces showing their concern.

"What the—?" Mr. Barnes said loudly as he rushed from next door to join the kids. "That boom sounded as if it came from nearby. What was it? Did a train derail or something?"

"I don't think so, Dad," David said.

The boy pointed south to the location of the train tracks that ran along Oakdale's southern edge.

"The tracks are southeast of here," David said, pointing. "But the explosion came from the northeast."

Mr. Barnes looked confused. "Are you sure about that, son? There's nothing much in that direction except farm country."

Joe's mother, Ellen Talbot, was the next to join them. She, too, had heard the explosion and had come running outside to investigate. But, like everyone else, she didn't know what had caused the noise.

Ellen looked concerned at first. Then she saw that Joe and his friends were perfectly safe.

"Joe?" Ellen asked. "What happened? What was that sound?"

David saw Joe shrug. "We don't know for sure, Mom," Joe answered, "but it sounded like something crashed. We think it may have been the green glow!"

"You mean it's back again?" someone asked in a high-pitched voice.

David turned and saw Wanda Gilmore rushing up the sidewalk. Her eyes were wide and bright with excitement. Wanda Gilmore was also a next-door neighbor to Joe and his mom.

She was dressed in one of her usual creative outfits: a pair of white Capri pants decorated with blue and green cartoon fish, along with a yellow-striped top and fluffy yellow slippers shaped like ducks. The owner and columnist for the town's only newspaper, *The Oakdale Chronicle*, Wanda had an endless appetite for all things that were strange and unexplained.

And UFOs were one of her many interests.

Though the first sighting of the green glow hadn't led to firm proof that aliens existed, Wanda continued to hold out hope. She seemed sure that one day, soon, extraterrestrials would show themselves to the human race—it was only a matter of time. Wanda had said she just hoped that they did it in Oakdale . . . so she could have the exclusive story for the *Chronicle.*

"Yes, Miss Gilmore," Joe told Wanda. "It rolled through the sky from the southwest to the northeast, then disappeared. A couple of seconds later we heard the explosion."

Wanda clapped her hands together in uncontrolled excitement. "My goodness!" she exclaimed. "Can it be? Do you think we've got a Roswell, New Mexico, all over again—right here in Oakdale?"

David shook his head, more than a little doubtful about the possibility. "Gee, Miss Gilmore," he said, "I don't think—"

"Roswell, New Mexico," Wanda went on dreamily, as though no one else had spoken. "Nineteen forty-seven! A mysterious aircraft crashes in the desert. . . ."

David knew the rest of the story, but he listened politely anyway. So did Joe and Sam.

"The local newspaper in New Mexico," Wanda went on, "reported that it was an alien spacecraft that had crashed, but the U.S. Army quickly stepped in and classified the whole incident as top-secret. The next thing anyone knew, the military said that what crashed was a weather balloon. But all the information on the incident has stayed under lock and key for more than fifty years!"

As if Wishbone understood what Wanda was saying, he shook himself and barked.

"Well," Joe said, "the only way we'll ever know what's going on is to go find the crash site and investigate!" He looked first at Sam, then at David, who certainly looked ready for an adventure.

Ellen looked at her wristwatch and shook her head. "I'd say it's much too late for the three of you to go off exploring by yourselves," she said.

"I agree," Mrs. Barnes told David. "Besides, if something did crash, the last thing the authorities need now is a bunch of people getting in their way. I'll call the police just in case they didn't hear or see the crash. You can go looking for the crash site tomorrow morning, all right?"

David was disappointed, but he didn't have much choice in the matter. "Okay, Mom," he said.

"I'm going with you," Wanda said quickly. "My reporter's instinct is twitching like crazy."

"I'm kind of curious, too," Joe's mom said. "Maybe I'll tag along, as well."

"I'd like to know what's going on out at the crash site myself," David's father said thoughtfully. His wife nodded in agreement.

Joe knelt down and gave Wishbone a couple of scratches behind his ears. "I guess that means you'll need to come along, too, boy! Who else is going to keep the rest of us out of trouble?"

Chapter Two

Wishbone was awake even before the sun rose. After all, he knew that Joe wanted to investigate the mysterious crash that had occurred the night before. The terrier certainly wasn't going to let Joe go anywhere without him.

Finally, Joe sat up in his bed. Even though he had tossed and turned all night, the boy didn't look sleepy at all. On the contrary, he was bright-eyed and excited. As Wishbone watched, his pal got out of bed and washed up in record time. Then Joe dressed and hurried downstairs to grab a quick breakfast. Naturally, the terrier raced down the stairs after him.

Joe's mom was already waiting for him in the kitchen. She stood at the stove, scrambling eggs. She had also filled Wishbone's food dish, a sight that he was happy to see.

"Ah," he said, following the aroma across the kitchen, "the kibble smells lovely this Sunday morning. My compliments to the chef."

"'Morning, Mom," said Joe.

"Good morning, Joe," Ellen replied. "How did you sleep?"

"Not so well," the boy told her. He sat down at the table. "I just couldn't stop thinking about what happened last night."

Ellen pointed to the portable television on the counter near the stove. "Same here," she confessed. "And we weren't the only ones who heard that noise. I was watching the early news before you came down. It seems the whole town heard it."

Ellen lifted the frying pan of eggs off the burner. She started to spoon them out onto two plates, which already held toast and bacon. "Apparently," she went on, sneaking a sideways look at her son, "something crashed on the old Blumenfeld farm just outside town."

"I knew it!" Joe said. "Did the news report say what it was?"

Ellen shook her head as she took the plates from the countertop and placed them on the table for herself and Joe. "The TV reporter handling the story didn't know," she told him. "It seems that the farm's been blocked off by a squad of security people. They're not releasing any details."

"That's weird," said Joe, "isn't it?" He picked up his fork. "I mean, if it was a car accident or an airplane crash or something like that, there wouldn't be any reason to keep it a secret, would there?"

"I can't imagine there would be," Ellen said. She sat down at the table across from Joe. "I have to agree with you. The way the situation is being handled does make it sound suspicious."

Joe dug into his food. He was clearly in a hurry to finish and be on his way.

"Slow down, Joe," Ellen advised him with a smile. "Whatever is happening out there on the farm isn't going anywhere."

Wishbone was watching Ellen and Joe finish their breakfast. Suddenly, he heard the sound of footsteps outside the kitchen door, followed by a rapid knocking. Before Ellen could answer, the door flew open and Wanda Gilmore came rushing in.

"Are we ready to go?" she asked, her voice quivering with excitement.

Wanda was dressed for serious reporting. She wore an old-style gray pinstriped suit with wide lapels over a white shirt and red tie. A gray fedora was perched on top of her head. A card that read "Press" was stuck in the hat's brim.

"Just about," Ellen said. "Would you like a cup of tea while we finish up?"

"No time for tea," Wanda announced. "This is the biggest story to hit Oakdale in a long time. I want to make sure the *Chronicle* doesn't miss out on it."

"Well, then," Ellen told her, exchanging a smile with Joe, "we'd better get going."

Joe got up and placed his breakfast plate in the sink. Then he turned to his mother. "Is it okay if I do the dishes when we get back from the crash site, Mom?"

"Yes! It's fine!" Wanda exclaimed. "I can't miss out on a scoop just because of some dirty dishes."

Ellen playfully ruffled Joe's hair. "You heard the lady," she said with a laugh. She picked up her purse and car keys from the counter and pointed to the door. "Let's move out, troops."

Joe looked at Wishbone. "You coming, boy?"

Wishbone raised himself onto all fours in no time.

"I'm with you, Joe." Then he led the way out the door to the Ford Explorer. Joe, Ellen, and Wanda were close on his tail. He threw them one last look over his shoulder. "Come on, everybody. Adventure awaits!"

As it turned out, Wishbone and his friends weren't the only ones traveling north that morning. It looked as though half of Oakdale was out investigating. It seemed the local television and radio news stations had made the crash a hot topic.

The closer Wishbone and his companions drove to the old Blumenfeld farm, the more upset Wanda became. "Oh, gosh," she muttered in the backseat of Ellen's vehicle. "I knew I should've done my investigation last night! Now everybody's here. There goes my exclusive!"

Wishbone did his best to calm her. He laid his chin on her lap and looked up at her with his big brown eyes. "Try scratching my ears," he said. "That always makes me feel better. Maybe it'll work for you, too."

By the time the group was within half a mile of the

old Blumenfeld farm, traffic had become too heavy for them to continue to drive. People were parking on the side of the road and finishing the trek on foot.

Wishbone stood on his hind legs and stuck his head out the opened vehicle window, examining the many scents floating on the air. "I don't smell any aliens out there," he told Joe. "It's safe to continue, people! But stay close to me."

With his three friends by his side, Wishbone joined the flow of the curious making their way to the farm. There was almost a carnival atmosphere to the morning. Something new and different had arrived in Oakdale, and many of the town's residents had come together to experience it.

There was also something reassuring about having the crowd to share this with. "After all," Wishbone said wisely, "there's safety in numbers."

In horror and science fiction movies, monsters and aliens usually attacked people when they were alone, in the dark of night or in some lonely spot. However, this was more of a party, and the area was crowded.

People were chatting happily and excitedly about the incident. Friends and neighbors were greeting one another as if they were taking a leisurely stroll in the countryside.

Wishbone wondered how many of these people believed they were on their way to see a crashed alien spacecraft. He knew that the last time the green glow had appeared in the skies over Oakdale, there had been a lot of talk about the subject.

That was when Gilbert Pickering, a boy Joe's age, had invited David to speak about aliens on the weekly local radio show he hosted at the WOAK studio. Then

Gilbert had sent David e-mail messages, claiming they were from an alien. In the end, of course, Gilbert's scheme had been exposed as an attempt to drum up interest in his show.

Gilbert also admitted that he had planted a piece of material marked with a bizarre-looking symbol to add to the drama of his hoax—but it had turned out to be some new scientific discovery his uncle was working on. For all the excitement stirred up by the green glow, it had come to nothing.

Except for the glow itself. That remained a mystery.

Just then, Wishbone and his group caught sight of David and his parents. "Hey!" said Wishbone. "We're over here!"

Joe waved, too. He caught his friend's attention. Seeing Joe, David pulled his parents over. As the adults greeted one another, Joe and David talked about the crash.

"You still sure there's no such thing as a UFO?" Joe asked playfully.

David sighed. "We'll find out soon enough. It's only a few hundred feet more to the crash site."

As an admirer of great literature, Wishbone knew a lot about UFOs from the books that he and Joe shared. Scary as it could be, UFOs were still a cool topic. It was fun to imagine that there might be other intelligent beings sharing the universe with dogs and humans.

Considering that there were trillions and trillions of stars in the universe, it made sense that some of them were circled by planets like Earth. In fact, astronomers had recently discovered as many as seventeen planets orbiting distant stars.

The terrier wondered what that life might be like. In science fiction novels, aliens were always trying to conquer Earth. But that was just make-believe, he reminded himself. If aliens were hostile and had been visiting Earth for years, wouldn't they have decided to attack a long time ago?

When Wishbone's group came within sight of the road to the Blumenfeld farm, they saw at least a dozen security people walking around and making sure that no one entered the farm. Then the terrier saw someone else—Sam, with her father. A moment later, the Keplers joined the group, too.

"Hi-ya, Sam," Joe said. "Good morning, Mr. Kepler."

"Hello, Joe," said Walter Kepler. He pointed ahead. "Some crowd this thing's attracted, isn't it?"

It was some crowd, all right. There were well over a hundred people milling around the road to the old, abandoned farm. Among them were parked a small group of television news vans, which had big satellite uplink dishes on their roofs.

There were reporters, as well, of course, both men and women. They were interviewing people in the crowd or speaking into microphones in front of video cameras.

"Look at all the reporters," Sam remarked, her eyes bright with excitement. "I guess this is a bigger story than we thought."

"They'll probably want to talk to me," Wishbone said. "Well, just tell them I'm still investigating and I'll have a full statement for them later." With that, the dog trotted off to check out the area, his nose to the ground as he searched for clues.

Wishbone knew most of the people who had gathered on the road since most of them had come from Oakdale. But news of the crash had spread far and wide, attracting a number of strangers to the area.

The terrier paid close attention to those newcomers.

Several of them were weird-looking enough to be aliens themselves, he thought.

"For instance," he said, eyeing a light-haired, bushy-browed man standing well apart from the crowd, "you look pretty suspicious to me. Everyone else is talking to someone, but you're trying awfully hard to stay by yourself. I wonder if you know something we don't . . . or if you're—*egads!*—one of *them!*"

As casually as he could, Wishbone trotted by the man. He tried to get a closer sniff of the stranger without being noticed. But the man saw the terrier approaching and took a few steps back.

"Aha!" said Wishbone. "So you *are* trying to hide something, Mr. Bushy-brows! Well, you can be sure this canine is going to keep a close eye on you!"

He looked around some more. His gaze finally fell on a short man with dark, curly hair and thick glasses. The fellow wore a rumpled brown suit. He was talking heatedly to one of the television reporters, his hands moving about wildly as he spoke.

"What do *you* have to say for yourself, sir?" Wishbone wondered.

Curious, he trotted off. When he was within hearing range, he sat down and listened to what the fellow was saying.

". . . just another attempt by the government to cover up the truth about UFOs," the man declared. "I have documented hundreds of cases of close encounters between mankind and alien visitors. But, as in this case, the authorities have gone to great lengths to keep the truth from the people. If this isn't the site of a UFO crash, why have they hushed it up? We have a right to know!"

Ah, Wishbone thought, *a true believer!* "Well," he

said, "everybody's got a right to believe whatever they want . . . but I sure hope he's wrong!"

The terrier spent a few more minutes nosing around the area. Then, certain there was no immediate danger to Joe and his friends, he headed back to where the group was standing.

"Whatever the story is," Mr. Kepler said, "someone sure is keeping it to themselves."

He pointed to the gate that closed off the dirt access road that led directly to the farm. Two more security men stood just inside the gate. They wore gray uniforms. They had holsters on their belts and walkie-talkies in their hands.

Their eyes were hidden behind dark sunglasses, but Wishbone could tell by the way they stood that they were looking around at the crowd. Their job was obvious—to keep everybody out. The men seemed even more mysterious because there were no identifying badges on their uniforms.

"Seems they're security guards," Sam's father said, "hired by the property's owners. They're not letting anybody in."

Wanda peered suspiciously at the security guards. "They can't keep me out. I'm with the press!"

Mr. Kepler said, "They haven't let the TV reporters in yet. I don't know if you'll have much luck."

"Well," said Wanda, "we'll just see about that." Squaring her shoulders, she marched confidently toward the gate, her reporting tools in hand.

One of the security guards held up his hand as she walked closer. "Sorry, ma'am," he said. "We've got strict orders not to let anybody in without permission from the owners."

Wanda pointed to the press card in the brim of her hat. "I'm with *The Oakdale Chronicle,* young man. I'd like to see the crash site."

The second guard shook his head. "I'm afraid that's not possible, ma'am."

"Well, then," Wanda demanded, "with whom do I have to speak to get permission?"

"I wouldn't know, ma'am," the first man said.

"Who are you working for, then?" she asked.

"The owners of the property, ma'am."

"And that would be . . . ?" Wanda inquired, her pen poised over her pad to take notes.

"We weren't given any names, ma'am," said the guard. "We were just told to watch this gate and keep it closed."

"*Someone* must be in charge!" Wanda said, losing her patience.

The second guard shrugged. "I wouldn't know, ma'am."

"Is your boss at the site of the UFO crash?" Wanda asked slyly, hoping to catch the man off guard.

But he wasn't so easy to trip up. "I don't know anything about a UFO, ma'am."

"It's common knowledge," Wanda said casually.

"The only thing we know," the first security guard said patiently, "is that we can't allow anyone to set foot on this property. It's for safety reasons."

"But can't I just—" Wanda started to plead.

The guard quickly said, "Sorry, ma'am. No one's allowed in." With that, he turned away from her and started to scan the crowd again.

Wanda stood there helplessly for several moments before snapping, "Oh, darn it all!" Frustrated by her failure to scoop a great story, she stormed away from the gate.

Wishbone didn't believe for a moment that Wanda was being kept away because of safety reasons. "More like a cover-up," he said, sympathizing with her frustration.

Wanda rejoined Joe and the others some distance from the gate.

"Well?" Joe asked. "What did they tell you?"

"Nothing!" Wanda fumed. "Something big is going on in there, and they're going to an awful lot of trouble to make sure we don't find out what it is!"

"Who's 'they'?" David asked.

Wanda shrugged. "The guards don't seem to know."

Joe, David, and Sam exchanged looks with one another. "Very mysterious," Sam said.

"It may be a mystery now," said Wanda, "but it's not going to remain one." She pointed a finger in the air and declared, "I'm on the job . . . and I am going to get answers—if it's the last thing I do!"

Wanda squinted her eyes as she studied the crowd.

"Somebody around here has to know something," she continued. "It's a reporter's job to dig up every bit of information and then feed it to the public."

Wanda stopped and pointed at the curly-haired man in the rumpled suit. He was no longer speaking with the TV reporter. Now he was talking about UFOs to a small group of people who had gathered around him.

"Now, that gentleman looks like he has something important to say," she observed. She went charging off to speak with him.

Wishbone and the kids followed her.

"Excuse me, sir," said Wanda, as she joined the cluster of people listening to the man. "My name's Wanda

26

Gilmore. I'm with *The Oakdale Chronicle*
know something about what's going on h(

"I most certainly do, Ms. Gilmore,"
grandly. "Of course, if you asked the au
what I know, they would tell you I was crazy!"

Wanda raised an eyebrow. "You're not . . . are you?"

"Indeed, not," he responded quickly. "My name is
Herbert Collier. I'm new in town—a visiting professor of
astrophysics at Oakdale College."

"Ah," said Wanda, smiling. "An expert! Just who I
need for my story."

Professor Collier smiled modestly. "I'm something
of an expert, yes," he admitted. "It would be my pleasure
to assist you any way I can."

"Well," Wanda began, "I'm sure you've heard all the
talk about the farm being the site of a UFO crash last
night—"

Professor Collier cut her off, his face growing serious.
"It's *more* than talk, Miss Gilmore." He waved his hand in
the direction of the security guards, blocking the entrance
to the farm. "I'm convinced that what those *ruffians* are
doing is covering up an extraterrestrial occurrence. A UFO
crash, you understand."

Joe and his friends were following the discussion
with great interest. Wishbone, on the other hand, had
heard the professor's story already.

"Please carry on, though," he said. "I'll be around if
you need me." The dog set off again, nose to the ground,
seeking whatever clues his talented and sensitive nose
might uncover.

He paid no attention to the gate that blocked the
way onto the old Blumenfeld farm. The guards didn't
even seem to notice him.

Here goes, the clever canine thought. . . . And he slipped past both the guards and the gate, leaving the crowd behind. No one had lived on the farm for several years. It was nothing more than an overgrown field now, stretched out in front of him like a big, exciting adventure.

"Hmm . . ." Wishbone said, as he wandered this way and that over the field, his nose gathering clues by the bushelful. "No unusual scents. In fact, it smells just like an old farm *should* smell."

Wishbone was an all-around detective. That meant he used his eyes, as well as his nose and ears. And what his eyes had zeroed in on was an area in the overgrown field where some of the weeds had been destroyed. Farther on, Wishbone could see more destruction—burnt trees and plants. He also saw and smelled some lingering smoke.

Wagging his tail, the terrier padded over to the weeds. As he got closer, he saw that the dirt had been overturned. "Did someone bury something here?" Wishbone asked himself. "Well, there's only one way to find out, and that's by doing one of the many things I do best—digging!"

With that, Wishbone reached for the soft ground with his front paws and began to shovel away. Dirt flew all around him, his forelegs a blur of motion. One thing the hours he had spent exploring the flower beds in Wanda's front garden had done was make him an expert at excavation—so it took him only a short time to unearth some evidence.

It was a piece of something hard and thin, almost eight inches square. It was slightly twisted and torn up, as though it had gone through a terrible time before it had been buried.

Then he saw something on the surface of it. It was an imprint—and, by golly, he had seen it before!

"I know this stuff!" Wishbone said in surprise. And he did. After all, he had dug up a piece of it from David's front lawn the last time the green glow had come to town!

Chapter Three

Being a dog of action, Wishbone knew that sitting there puzzling over the object was a waste of time. "Joe's going to want to see this for sure," he said. Grabbing the thing in his teeth, he ran back in the direction from which he had come.

When he got to the gate, he saw that the security guards were still standing watch. But once again, the two men didn't even glance in his direction as he silently slithered past them.

Undercover Dog Wishbone is about to make his way through enemy lines! he thought. Then he ducked beneath the gate to join the crowd still gathered on the farm's approach road.

The terrier looked around for Joe, but he didn't see his friend anywhere. He didn't see David and Sam either. Ellen, Mr. Kepler, and the Barneses were still there, however.

"Guess they must've headed to the cars," said Wishbone. "Well, they may have a head start, but I've got something to make up for that—four legs to their two!"

With that, Wishbone started down the road in a

trot. In just a few minutes, he saw Joe, David, and Sam walking along ahead of him. Speeding up his pace, he caught up with them.

"Hey, you guys!" Wishbone said. "Look what I found!"

They didn't seem to hear him.

"Oh, wait," Wishbone said, racing ahead of them and letting the object in his mouth drop to the ground at their feet. "How rude of me to talk with my mouth full! As I was saying . . ."

"Hi, Wishbone," Joe said. "Guess you got tired of waiting around for nothing, too, huh?"

"Not exactly," Wishbone said, touching the square object with his paw. "Look what I dug up."

"Hey . . . what's this?" David asked. His eyes flashed with excitement as he caught sight of the fragment. He leaned over and picked it up, inspecting it closely. "Oh, wow! Do you know what this looks like?"

"Like that piece of silver-looking material I dug up from your lawn last year," Wishbone answered.

Joe took it from David, while Sam looked curiously over his shoulder. "Yeah," he said. "It's kind of beat up, but other than that, it looks like that piece of silver-looking stuff that Wishbone dug up from your lawn last year."

"Just like I said," Wishbone told them, wagging his tail in triumph. "No one ever listens to the dog."

Joe knelt down beside Wishbone. "Where did you find this, boy?"

The terrier said, "Buried on the farm. Finding it wasn't anything anyone with a superior nose couldn't have done."

David took the specimen back from Joe and examined

31

it some more. "It's covered with dirt, as if it's been buried in the ground." He looked at his friends, a thoughtful expression on his face. "Probably somewhere on the farm. Wishbone could've sneaked right past the security guards and found it there. And the way it's chewed up and twisted—"

"Like it was in some kind of crash?" Sam said breathlessly.

Eyes wide, the three friends exchanged questioning looks.

"Wait a second," Joe said. "The last time we saw this kind of material—"

". . . was the last time we saw the green glow," Sam blurted out, finishing her friend's thought. "Gilbert admitted that he buried it under David's lawn as part of his UFO hoax."

"Right," Joe said. "He got it from his uncle, who's a research scientist who developed the stuff for the space program."

"But Gilbert told us his uncle only had the one piece to lend out," Sam noted. "So where did *this* one come from?"

"That's what I'd like to know," Wishbone chimed in.

"I think that's a question we've got to ask Gilbert," David said.

As David handed Gilbert Pickering the twisted piece of material in the living room of Gilbert's house, it was clear that Gilbert was amazed. "Wow!" he said. "Where did you get this?"

"We thought maybe *you* might know," David said.

32

"Me? How would I know?" the blond-haired boy with eyeglasses asked in surprise.

Sam, who was down on one knee, smiled as she scratched Wishbone behind the ears. "Well," she said, "it wouldn't be the first time you tried to pull a fast one on us. Weren't you the guy who buried phony evidence of a UFO for us to find?"

Gilbert waved his hand before him. "If you're suggesting that I would be so unimaginative as to repeat a hoax, let me be the first to tell you that that isn't the way I work. Besides," he said with a sly smile at David, "I know better than to match wits with my friend Mr. Barnes here. He found me out much too easily when I pulled my little prank."

"It wasn't that easy, Gilbert," David said. "You almost had me believing I was communicating with an alien by e-mail. If I didn't know a little about writing computer programs, I never would have been able to trace those

e-mails back to your computer. You sure had me fooled for a while."

"Well, anyway, you guys are my friends now," Gilbert assured them. "I wouldn't pull any tricks on you. Besides, the only reason I did it last time was to drum up interest for my program."

He was referring to *Youth Viewpoint,* the weekly half-hour show he hosted on WOAK, the local radio station.

"After what happened last time," said Gilbert, "I'm not about to do another show on UFOs and aliens. I think my credibility on that topic is kind of shot."

"Then how do you explain finding this fragment near the crash site?" Joe wondered.

"I can't," Gilbert said. His eyes flashed bright and he smiled. "But maybe my uncle can!"

David remembered what Gilbert had told them about his uncle. "He works for Littleton Aerospace, doesn't he?" the boy asked.

Gilbert nodded. "That's right. I'll call him tonight to find out if we can visit and ask him a few questions."

"Great," David said. "Then maybe we'll get to the bottom of this whole mystery!"

Wishbone wagged his tail as if he was just as excited about the idea as the rest of them.

Joe was just starting to get dressed the next morning when he heard his mother calling him from downstairs.

"Joe! It's David on the phone for you."

Joe pulled his T-shirt over his head as he hurried down the steps. He raced into the kitchen and took the telephone from his mom. Wishbone was right behind him, as always.

"Hi, David," he said. "What's up?"

"I just spoke to Gilbert," David said, his voice full of excitement. "He talked to his uncle last night, just as he promised. He said he would be happy to have us come out to his office and visit him—this afternoon, if we want."

"Great!" Joe said. "Is it okay with your folks if you go?"

"Yes," David replied. "And Sam's father gave his permission, too. How about you?"

"Wait a minute," Joe said. He put his hand over the phone and turned to his mother. "Mom, Gilbert's uncle invited us to come out to Littleton Aerospace this afternoon. Is that all right?"

Ellen placed the plate with Joe's breakfast on the table. "As long as he's sure you kids won't be getting in his way, it's fine with me."

Joe smiled at her. "Thanks, Mom." Then he spoke into the phone again. "We're set!" he told his friend.

"Excellent," David said. "I've always been curious about what goes on at an aerospace company, anyway. No matter what we learn about the green glow and the silver-looking object, this should be a very interesting experience."

They said their good-byes. Then Joe hung up the phone and joined his mother at the kitchen table for breakfast.

"What do *you* think is going on?" Joe asked his mother.

"Oh," she said, "I'm sure there's a logical explanation for everything."

A librarian at the Henderson Memorial Public Library,

Ellen Talbot was a sensible and rational woman. She was, in some ways, a lot like David Barnes, Joe thought—slow to jump to conclusions. She demanded solid evidence and hard facts before making a decision.

Joe's mom thoughtfully buttered a slice of toast. "I don't suppose I would be surprised if there were other beings in the universe," she said, setting her butter knife down. "I just find it strange that after fifty years of UFO reports and so-called close encounters with aliens, nobody has ever come up with absolute proof that extraterrestrials have been visiting us."

"That's how I feel," Joe said. "Of course, some people would say that the reason we don't have proof is because there's a plot involving the United States government to keep the evidence secret." He laughed, then drank some milk. "You know, I've been reading another one of those old mystery novels of Dad's," he said. "It's called *The Assassination Bureau,* and it's written by the author Jack London."

"Yes," Ellen said, smiling at the memory of her husband. "Your father loved Jack London's books. But I didn't know he wrote mystery novels. I thought he just wrote adventure stories that took place in areas like the Klondike and the South Pacific."

"Well," said Joe, "this one's a mystery. It's about a man named Dragomiloff, and he's behind some kind of conspiracy. But I only just started it last night before going to bed, so I haven't gotten very far into it." He smiled. "I'm as confused by Dragomiloff's plans as I am about the green glow. I wonder which mystery I'll get the solution to first."

"Maybe I'm being a bit naïve," his mom responded, "but something tells me the explanation to your real-life mystery is a lot simpler than any mystery you'll find in a book."

"Maybe," Joe said. He looked at Wishbone, who was lying at his feet, his tail wagging. Then he looked out the window.

Or maybe not, he thought.

Chapter Four

Littleton Aerospace was a big complex of buildings about twenty miles outside Oakdale. The company's offices and laboratories were in a long line of low, red-brick buildings. They were flanked by airplane hangars on one side, and a landing field on the other. The entire complex was surrounded by a tall, chain-link fence.

The only way in was through a single gate. It stood at the end of a narrow, two-lane road that branched off the highway. There was a large guardhouse next to the gate, and a heavy barricade lowered across the entry road. Two uniformed security guards stood watch over the entrance.

"Pretty serious-looking," David whispered to his friends in the backseat of Gilbert's uncle's car.

"Just like the guards at the crash site," Joe whispered back.

Wishbone, who was sitting in Joe's lap, just wagged his tail.

Gilbert's uncle had driven into Oakdale during his lunch hour to pick up his nephew, along with Joe, David,

Sam, and Wishbone. Although the terrier hadn't really been invited, Gilbert's uncle hadn't objected when the dog jumped into the backseat and settled down for the trip.

"Thanks again for letting us visit, Uncle Max," Gilbert said, as the guards lifted the barricade and waved them through the open gate.

"Yes, Dr. Pickering," Joe said. "We know how busy you must be."

It seemed to David that there was a strong family resemblance between Gilbert and his uncle. Like his nephew, Max Pickering was blond and wore glasses. They seemed to be good friends, as well, and shared an interest in the sciences.

"I'm not very busy Monday afternoons," Max Pickering told them. "Besides, I can always find time for my favorite nephew. And call me 'Max,' will you? 'Doctor' makes it sound like I'm going to check your pulse instead of giving you a guided tour."

David chuckled. "So . . . what kind of degree do you have, Dr. Pick—er . . . I mean, Max?"

"Technically," said Gilbert's uncle, "I'm an aeronautical engineer. That means I help design aircraft. But here at Littleton, I specialize in metallurgy."

"Metallurgy," Sam said. "That's the study of metals, right?"

"More or less," Max said, as he eased his car into a parking spot marked with his name. It was right next to the largest building on the Littleton grounds. "My specialty is developing new metals and other materials for the aerospace industry."

Joe said, "You mean like that piece of material you lent to Gilbert that he tried to convince us was from another planet?"

"Hmm . . . yes," Max said, giving Gilbert a stern look. "He got a good talking to when I discovered that was what he used the material for. I thought he was going to be using it in a science project for school."

Gilbert smiled sheepishly. "I've learned the error of my ways, Uncle Max. I promise."

"Good!" said his uncle.

A moment later, Max Pickering turned off the engine and everyone piled out of the car. "Anyway," he told the kids, "that material's an excellent example of what I do here. It was developed to be lightweight, yet strong and capable of withstanding extremely high temperatures."

"Sounds like it would be useful in building airplanes and rockets," David said, nodding. "Has it been used for anything like that yet?"

Max shook his head. "Sorry, David. We have contracts with the military and NASA here. A lot of the work we do is classified, top-secret information. I'm afraid I can't answer all of your questions."

"Oh, we understand," David said. But he was a little disappointed by the man's answer. If Gilbert's uncle wasn't going to answer their questions because the information was "classified," they were never going to learn anything.

Max directed the group through the front doors of the building. They were marked with a sign that said "Engineering."

Once inside, they came to the reception area. There, Max signed the kids in as his guests. They were each issued a temporary peel-and-stick name tag that they were warned not to remove while inside the building. Wishbone, of course, didn't need a temporary name tag. He already had a permanent one—worn on his collar.

Telling everyone to stick close by him, Max took the

group through a set of sliding doors into Littleton Aero-space's engineering department.

Doors were set every few yards on either side of the quiet, whitewashed corridors. Next to most of the doors was a large plate-glass window that allowed them to look into the rooms the doors led to.

David saw that each room was a laboratory specializing in a particular project or problem. So each room was set up with a special kind of scientific equipment. Some labs, however, had blinds drawn over their windows for what Max called "security reasons."

He told the kids that even *he* didn't know what the scientists in those rooms were working on. "Like I said," he remarked, "we're big on classified information around here."

David was wide-eyed with curiosity. He had always been interested in science, ever since he was little. This was just the kind of place he had hoped to work in when he grew up. Finally getting to see the large range of possi-bilities was making his mouth water in anticipation.

It wasn't Gilbert's first visit to Littleton, so he didn't seem to be quite as impressed. However, David was willing to bet that his friend was just keeping his excitement under control.

Finally, after more than half an hour, Max took the kids and Wishbone into his own laboratory. He put on a white lab coat. "I'm afraid what I do here is not as inter-esting or glamorous as building Martian landrovers or deep-space probes," he said apologetically, as he ushered the kids into his work space. "But I call it home."

The room was a medium-sized lab that held several workbenches and stools. Each workbench was covered with a collection of beakers containing boiling chemical solutions. Curved-glass tubes full of mysterious gases and strangely colored fluids connected one beaker to another.

Against the far wall stood several kilns—special small, high-powered ovens used to bake and harden ceramics. Little red lights glowed on their doors to show they were in use. Another workbench held a wide variety of tools for cutting, drilling, and shaping. David might have found such items in any home workshop.

"Right now," Max said, as the kids spread out to look at his setup, "I'm working on creating new compounds with ceramics and polymers."

David glanced at him. "You mean creating heavy molecular chains by chemically combining two or more molecules of the same kind?"

"Er . . . why, yes, exactly," Max Pickering said, taking off his glasses and looking at David in surprise.

"I warned you about David, Uncle Max," Gilbert said with a laugh. "He's pretty smart. As a matter of fact, I'd watch out for him if I were you. He'll probably be after your job by the time we graduate from high school!"

"I don't think so," David said, embarrassed by Gilbert's praise.

"I wouldn't be surprised if Gilbert was right," Max said, as he sat down on one of the stools. "Not many kids your age know much about polymers. Anyway, Gilbert tells me you kids have some questions for me. About the UFO crash the other night, right?"

David was staring at a beaker full of chemicals. At the mention of a UFO, however, his head whipped around. "You . . . you mean you're admitting that what crashed out there at the Blumenfeld farm *was* a UFO?"

"Whoa! Not so fast," Max said with a laugh. He held

out his hand like a traffic cop. "I said 'UFO,' not 'alien spacecraft'!"

"What's the difference?" Sam asked.

"In aeronautics," said Max, "we use the term 'UFO' for any object that we can't identify, even other aircraft. But with all the rumors about alien visits and such in recent years, everybody immediately jumps to the conclusion that 'UFO' refers to an alien flying saucer."

Max rose and walked over to a desk shoved into a corner of the room. On it sat a computer terminal almost buried in mountains of papers, scientific journals, files, and computer printouts. He began to sort through the papers as he continued to talk to the kids.

"What came down on that farm two nights ago was a UFO to you," Max remarked, "but not to us. In fact, Littleton is responsible for the crash."

"You *what?*" Joe blurted out.

David frowned. For a split-second, he had been willing to accept the word of a respected scientist that a UFO—an alien spaceship—had actually crashed near his hometown. He was almost disappointed to learn that hadn't been the case, after all.

"That's right, Joe," said Gilbert's uncle. "You see, what crashed was the model for a new kind of weather balloon developed for the air force. We had launched it for a test flight."

The man continued to search his desk.

"The weather was clear the other night, making it perfect for the balloon's first flight. Unfortunately, it ran into some unexpectedly strong winds. Those fierce winds ended up pushing the balloon rather quickly across the sky."

"That's why it seemed to be self-propelled?" asked David.

Max Pickering nodded. "Exactly." Finally finding the folder he wanted, he turned back to the kids. "Then the balloon developed some sort of malfunction that caused it to explode. It then came down on the old Blumenfeld farm."

"If it was just a weather balloon," Sam asked, "why all the security guards and secrecy?"

Max shook his head and sighed. "I told you—it's a military project. Sometimes the air force gets a little . . . overly cautious about security."

He opened the folder and pulled out an eight-by-ten color photograph. Then he held it up to show the kids a picture of a car-sized gondola, or passenger's basket, attached to a balloon about three times its size.

David could also estimate the size of the balloon by the men in air force uniforms and white laboratory coats surrounding it. But the most striking thing about it was its color.

"Hey! It's green," Joe pointed out.

"And shiny-looking," Sam added.

"The green glow in the sky!" David concluded.

"Exactly," Max Pickering told them. He smiled, putting down the first photograph. "It's made of the material that those shiny birthday balloons are made of. On a clear, bright night like that of the crash, a balloon made of that substance would have been visible for miles around."

"Where are the remains of the balloon now?" asked Gilbert.

"Over in one of the hangars," said his uncle. "Unfortunately, I can't show it to you. There are other top-secret items in there. You understand, don't you?"

"Sure," said Gilbert.

David exchanged looks with Joe and Sam. Something about what Dr. Pickering had just told them didn't sound right to him. He tried to remember how quickly the green glow had crossed the sky.

"Could the wind really have pushed a balloon *that* quickly?" he asked abruptly.

Max looked at him. "I wouldn't have thought so, either, but there you have it."

While David thought about his answer, the scientist reached into the pocket of his white lab coat and pulled out a package of chewing gum. Then he held it out to David and the others.

"Anyone care for a piece?" he asked.

David looked at the package with curiosity. Its size and shape were ordinary enough, but the color of the package was a red-yellow-and-black plaid that he had never seen before.

"Uh . . . no, thanks," Joe said, scrunching his nose.

"Same here," said David.

"Thanks, anyway," Sam added, turning her head away.

Max shrugged, took out a piece, and popped it into his mouth. Then he started to chew.

Whew! David thought. *That gum smells like some fancy kind of soap.* And by the expressions on his friends' faces, they also found the odor offensive. *Yuck!*

If it *smelled* that bad, he told himself, he could only imagine how awful it would taste. He couldn't believe anyone would want to chew something like that.

"So," said Gilbert, "if that weather balloon's so top-secret, Uncle Max, how come you're telling us about it?"

His uncle smiled. "The air force just this morning decided to declassify the project and the crash. Seems all the curiosity about the green glow and the balloon was

46

more trouble than keeping the project secret was worth. The Pentagon will release a statement this evening, along with this photo."

He flipped through some other pictures in the folder and pulled out another one. It showed an aerial view of the crash site.

"This is the first official shot of the crash," said the scientist.

Joe smiled at Sam and David. "Boy," he said, "imagine what Wanda would give to be here for this news scoop!"

"Who's Wanda?" Max asked.

"My neighbor, Wanda Gilmore. She's the owner and publisher of *The Oakdale Chronicle*," Joe told him.

"Well, have her call me," Max said. "I can give her the story this afternoon, so she can get a jump on the other papers and TV news reports."

"I sure will!" Joe said happily. "Thanks a lot!"

David knew that his friend was right. Wanda would love to get such a hot scoop for the *Chronicle*. And if Joe gave it to her, it might make up a little for all the times Wishbone had dug up her flower beds.

And speaking of the terrier . . . David looked around, but Joe's dog was nowhere to be seen.

"Hey," David asked, "have any of you seen Wishbone?"

"Phew!" Wishbone said, as he began to trot up the corridor, away from Max Pickering's laboratory. "Dr. P. is a nice enough guy, I guess, but he's got some terrible taste in chewing gum. If I didn't get out of that room, the scent would have knocked me out of my socks—that is, if I . . . wore socks."

Wishbone poked his head into the laboratory next to Max's.

"Well," he said, "since I'm out here, anyway, I may as well see what kind of cool stuff is going on in these other labs."

But in the first room he peeked into, nothing was going on. The lab was bare, as though it had recently been emptied and cleaned.

The door to the next laboratory was closed. Wishbone had to raise himself up on his hind legs and peer through the narrow slit between the bottom of the window and the drawn blinds. This room was empty of workers and only dimly lit, but it was full of equipment—the purpose of which Wishbone couldn't begin to understand.

He was about to get down and look for excitement elsewhere when something on the far side of the laboratory caught his eye. It was a figure, standing against the wall.

A figure? he thought, his heart racing. Looking more closely, the dog saw that it was about three feet tall, with an enormous round head and huge, glowing black eyes.

Wishbone gulped with a combination of excitement and fear. *Can it be?* he asked himself.

Had he actually found . . . an *alien?*

Chapter Five

"Okay, Wishbone," the Jack Russell terrier told himself. "Let's just stay calm here. It looks like an alien, all right . . . and it's looking right at me, so the alien knows I've seen *it*."

Wishbone kept his eyes locked on the little figure on the other side of the glass. After a few moments, he realized that the alien hadn't moved a muscle—hadn't so much as blinked, in fact, since being spotted. It was as though it were frozen in place with fear.

Maybe the alien is more afraid of me than I am of it, Wishbone thought. He glanced quickly up and down the corridor, scarcely daring to look away from his discovery. He was alone. With a being from another planet!

The dog looked back at the alien. Was it his imagination, or did the creature look a little frightened? *If it was going to do anything to hurt me,* the terrier thought, *it probably would have done it by now.*

"I sure can't blame the alien for being scared," Wishbone said. "The poor creature is millions of miles away from its home and family."

Wishbone knew he should go for help, but he didn't want to risk losing sight of the little alien. He had thought there was something fishy about Dr. Pickering's answers about UFOs, and now he was sure of it. Cornering this little extraterrestrial would prove that once and for all.

Taking a deep breath, Wishbone decided to take a chance and go face to face with the alien. He dropped down on all fours and hurried to the laboratory door. Then he pushed at it with his nose. The door, which had been slightly ajar, started to open wide.

"Hello," Wishbone called. He cautiously stuck his nose inside the lab. "I come in peace on behalf of all mankind . . . er, make that dogkind, too. Let me take you to my leader—or at least to my best friend, Joe."

The lab was silent. Wishbone sniffed carefully, but all he could smell was the odor of old chemicals. *Of course,* he thought, *for all I know, that's what aliens smell like!*

He placed one paw inside the room, then another. The alien was waiting against the far wall, opposite the door. Wishbone would have to walk around a workbench before the little alien would come into view.

As Wishbone padded across the floor, he held his ears straight up, on high alert for the slightest sound. As much as he believed he was in no danger from the extraterrestrial, he wasn't taking any unnecessary chances. It was better to be safe than sorry, he reminded himself.

Finally, he came to the edge of the workbench. Cautiously peeking around it, he got ready to face the visitor from another world. . . .

But when he took a closer look, he realized he wasn't gazing upon a real, live alien after all. He was staring at a poster tacked to the laboratory wall!

I knew that! Wishbone thought sheepishly. He walked over to the poster and sat down in front of it. "Thought you could fool me, huh?" he asked the figure in the picture. "Well, okay . . . you did. But only for a minute. I never really believed you were real."

He had to admit, however, that the figure shown on the poster was pretty realistic. From a distance, in poor light, it was understandable that even he could have been fooled.

Still, he was happy there weren't any witnesses to his "close encounter." He would have been embarrassed for anyone to have seen how easily he had been fooled.

Just then, the lights snapped on and he heard Joe say, "So, this is where you've gone!"

Wishbone turned and saw Joe, David, Sam, Gilbert,

and Dr. Pickering standing in the doorway. "Er . . . hi, guys," he said.

Joe shook his head. "You really shouldn't go wandering off by yourself, Wishbone. This is a high-security place and it could be dangerous."

"Blame it on Dr. Pickering's chewing gum," Wishbone said. "I had to get away from that smell."

He looked back at the alien poster. For the first time, he noticed that there was something else on the wall next to it. It was a large star chart, a map of the heavens, with a single star on it circled in red marker.

Wishbone peered closer at it and saw that the star was labeled "Sirius." *Hmm . . . the dog thought, I wonder what that's all about.*

Before he could investigate further, Joe knelt beside him and scooped him up off the floor. "C'mon, boy," he said.

"He sure seemed interested in the poster," David observed. He walked across the room and looked at the poster and then at the chart. "Sirius?" the boy asked. "Is this part of some research project?" he asked Gilbert's uncle.

"Uh . . . no," Max Pickering said quickly. "No, of course not. It's nothing. Just a silly hobby of one of my coworkers."

"Nothing you take very 'siriusly,' huh, Uncle Max?" Gilbert joked.

To Wishbone, the man's smile seemed strained. "He sure sounds nervous talking about something that's supposed to be silly," the terrier noted.

"Come on, everyone," Dr. Pickering said. "We really shouldn't be in here at all. Let's go back to my lab, okay?"

The kids followed the scientist out of the laboratory

and waited while he locked the door behind them. But just before the group left the room, Wishbone took one last, long look behind him at the star chart.

Something about this doesn't smell right to this canine, he thought suspiciously. *And I don't just mean the guy's chewing gum!*

Half an hour later, the kids' tour of Littleton Aerospace was over. After turning in their visitors' passes at the receptionist's desk in the lobby, David and the others followed Max Pickering outside to his car. He had offered to drive them back into town. Then he would return to work.

David got into the backseat first. Then came Sam and Joe. Wishbone piled in last of all and sat on Joe's lap, his tail wagging excitedly. Max sat in the front with his uncle.

As the car steered through the front gates, the terrier took a last look back at Littleton Aerospace—its buildings and its hangars. He decided that there was more to the place than met the eye.

Judging from the look on David's face, the boy had come to the same conclusion.

Chapter Six

As Wishbone sat in Joe's lap and watched the scenery go by, the terrier realized that he had quite a lot to think about.

For instance . . . why in the world had Dr. Pickering seemed so nervous about the kids seeing that star chart? It didn't seem as if there was anything special about it. It looked as if it had been torn out of a magazine.

"And you can probably buy that poster of the alien anywhere," the terrier said, thinking like a great detective—which he was. "So what's the big secret?" he asked himself.

As they pulled into town, Wishbone got an urge to visit his friend Sparky, the golden retriever.

Not only was Sparky fun to play chase with, the terrier thought happily, but he also usually had some great goodies in his dog dish. "And since today is good ol' Sparky's birthday," Wishbone said, "I bet there'll be some extra-special taste treats on hand for the celebration!"

Of course, Wishbone had to wait until Max Pickering pulled his car up to Joe's driveway before he could get out. But as soon as the door was open, he headed for his friend's house.

"Is your dog all right on his own?" Max asked Joe, loud enough for the terrier to hear.

"It's okay," Joe answered. "Wishbone's always going off on his own. He can find his way back home from anywhere."

"He'll be home in time for dinner, I bet," said Sam. "That's one dog who never misses a meal."

"Besides," said Joe, "everybody within miles of Oakdale knows Wishbone. He's got friends everywhere."

"You're not kidding," said Wishbone, as he trotted away to see one of them.

Unlike people in their cars, Wishbone could make his way around by using more than just roads and highways. He took a shortcut through a field of wild grass. Then he paused by a small stream that ran in a crooked course across the field. There, he took a break to lap up some of the cool, clear water. When his thirst was satisfied, he continued on his way.

"There's definitely something strange going on with Dr. Pickering," the terrier decided. "He's hiding something . . . and I bet the kids think so, too."

He noticed that they hadn't even asked the scientist about the silver material that Wishbone had found near the crash site. He probably would have taken it away from them if they had shown it to him.

"And then we would have been missing a valuable piece of evidence!" Wishbone declared.

At the far end of the field was a road. After looking both ways to make sure there wasn't any traffic, the terrier passed the library. He entered a wooded area between the road and a street of houses on the far side.

"Definitely something to think about," the terrier said, referring to what he had seen at Littleton Aerospace.

Emerging from the thin area of woods, he turned onto a short street with small, neatly kept houses. The houses had well-tended patches of lawn and attractive flower beds.

Normally, Wishbone would have chosen the best mound of flowers and spent some quality time digging beneath them to see what he might find. But today he was in a hurry to see Sparky. He decided to pass the flowers by. Instead, he went around to the rear of the house, where his four-legged buddy lived.

"Hey, there," Wishbone called, as he rounded the house and trotted into the backyard. Sparky's doghouse, a miniature replica of the big house that his people lived in, sat in the rear corner of the yard. "Oh, birthday dog! Are you there?"

No answer. Wishbone knew it possible Sparky was asleep in the cool darkness of the doghouse.

"It's a hot afternoon, after all," the terrier told himself. "Any self-respecting dog should be napping the day away."

Wishbone stuck his head inside the opening and looked around. Sparky wasn't home, but there was still something to see.

"Well, well, what do we have here?" the terrier asked. "A brand-new fire-hydrant chew toy and . . . oh, this is very nice! A new food dish! And not one of those cheap ones, either. This is quality stuff, with plenty of yummy goodies filling it to the brim! Looks like Sparky's having a great birthday."

As Wishbone backed out of the doghouse, he heard a low, irritated whimper behind him. Looking over his shoulder, he saw Sparky standing across the yard, staring at him. Sparky, a tall, lean golden retriever, was usually a happy, friendly dog, always glad to see his friend.

"Hey, Sparky, old pal," Wishbone greeted him happily. "Happy birthday! Looks like your people came through with some great gifts."

But Sparky didn't answer. He just looked at Wishbone as he held his ears back and let his tail swish anxiously.

Wishbone was confused. "Er . . . have I come at a bad time?" he asked.

The other dog circled around his friend. He edged his way past Wishbone and sat down hard at the entrance of the doghouse.

"What's wrong, Sparky?" Wishbone asked. "Having a bad birthday? What do you say we chow down on some of the food you've got in that new bowl of yours? . . . Oh, and by the way, Sparky, have I mentioned how nice the bowl is?"

Sparky still didn't answer. He also didn't move, as

though his only interest was guarding the door to his doghouse.

Wishbone snuffled. "I don't know what's gotten into you today," he told Sparky. "But if that's the way you're going to be about it, I may as well just trot on home."

The golden retriever lay down on his belly and whimpered, but he made no move to stop his visitor from leaving.

"Okeydokey, then," Wishbone said. "I guess I'll be going. See you around." He turned and trotted away.

Before the terrier disappeared around the side of the house, he stopped and took a last look back. But Sparky hadn't moved.

Hmm . . . Wishbone thought. *This isn't like Sparky. I've never seen him act in such a way. I wonder if he's in some kind of trouble. . . . If he is, why won't he tell me, his best friend?*

Knowing there was nothing he could do for Sparky until his friend decided to share his troubles with him, Wishbone headed home.

Chapter Seven

"No offense," David told Gilbert as Wishbone walked into the room, "but I don't think your uncle was telling us the truth."

Along with Joe and Sam—and now Wishbone, too—the boys were sitting around the Talbots' kitchen table. They were enjoying a snack while they discussed their visit to Littleton Aerospace.

Wishbone stood on his hind legs and tapped Joe's leg with his front paw. The boy laughed.

"Snack time?" he asked.

The terrier just looked at him.

Joe scratched Wishbone on the head and then held out a ginger snap for him. The dog took it in his teeth. Then he dropped back to the floor to eat.

"So, David," said Sam, picking up the conversation, "you think Dr. Pickering was lying to us?"

The boy shrugged. "I don't know what to think." He leaned his elbows on the table and dropped his chin into his hands. "After all, I saw the green glow both times it appeared. I'm almost positive that it wasn't a weather

59

balloon. It was moving through the sky much too quickly, and it seemed to be operating under its own power."

"Come on," Gilbert said. "Uncle Max showed us pictures of the balloon and the crash, didn't he?"

"Well, that's true," Sam said slowly. "But even if what we saw the other night *was* a weather balloon, like he said, that still doesn't explain the green glow we saw last year!"

"That's right," Joe chimed in. "Dr. Pickering said this was the balloon's first test flight! So what's his explanation for what we saw last year?"

Gilbert shook his head forcefully from side to side. "There's no way my uncle would lie to me. You don't know him the way I do."

"But he said it himself," David insisted. "The scientists at Littleton do a lot of classified work for the military. Maybe he didn't *want* to lie. But if what we saw by accident was top-secret, he wouldn't have any choice. He'd have to tell us a cover story."

"But you don't know it was a cover story," Gilbert said sullenly.

"Well, we do know that it sounds really fishy," Sam commented.

Joe nodded. "And did anyone notice how nervous he got when we asked him about that star chart in the laboratory Wishbone wandered into?"

"Yeah," David said. "He sure was jumpy, considering it was something he said was a joke!"

Gilbert groaned and folded his arms across his chest. "I really don't like all this talk," he said. "Uncle Max and I have always been close friends. I can't believe he would lie to me."

"He may not have had any choice, Gilbert," Sam pointed out.

"Which star was circled?" Joe asked.

"Sirius," David said. "Why?"

Joe shrugged. "Maybe we should check it out. You know, let's try to find out what's so interesting about that particular star."

"Good idea," David told him. "Let's hit the Net!"

The kids and Wishbone left Joe's house and walked next door to where David lived. After all, he had a computer in his bedroom. It didn't take long for the boy to boot it up and log onto the Internet.

Then he typed the name "Sirius" into the search engine. Everyone glued their eyes to the screen, waiting until a list of options appeared.

"I'll start with General Information," David told his friends.

He pointed the arrow at the proper line and clicked on the mouse. The computer whirred as it ran the search. Then the screen filled with words.

"Let's see," David said, reading to his friends. "Sirius, known as 'the dog star' . . ."

"I bet Wishbone likes it already," Sam chuckled.

David went on. ". . . because of its location in the constellation Canis Major, which is Latin for 'greater dog.' It's a southern constellation, visible in the Northern Hemisphere only from November to April."

"It says that the Egyptians called it Sothis," Sam added, reading over David's shoulder.

"The name 'Sirius' comes from a Greek word meaning 'scorching,'" David noted, "because it's such a bright star. In fact, it's the brightest in the whole night sky."

"It's located eight-point-seven light-years away from

Earth," Gilbert said, his eyes narrowed in interest. "That makes it one of the closest stars in the galaxy to our solar system."

A light-year was the distance light could travel in a year, David reminded himself. "That means the image of Sirius we see in the sky is almost nine years old by the time we see it," he said. He shrugged his shoulders. "Still, eight-point-seven light-years is pretty close to Earth."

Gilbert agreed. "Especially when you consider that with the Hubble space telescope in orbit around the Earth, astronomers have been able to look at objects well over eleven million light-years away."

Sam shook her head in astonishment. "So Sirius is, relatively speaking, really just next door to us?"

"Funny you should say that, Sam," David told her. "Check this out."

He had gone back to the list of Web sites that the search engine had located. He was pointing to one of them. It read: "The Dog Star: Our Neighbors in Space."

"Let's see what this is all about," David said.

He clicked on the name and waited for the Web page to come up. It opened with the title, under which was a painted picture of an alien being.

The kids exchanged looks of surprise. Even Wishbone, who had taken up a comfortable spot on David's bed, cocked his head as he looked at the computer screen.

"That's the same picture that was on the laboratory wall," David whispered, his heart beating hard in his chest.

"Yeah!" Joe said. "Spooky!"

David tried to stay calm. "Let's scroll down," he said, "and see what else there is here."

Once again, he read out loud. "Hmm . . ." he said,

"here's something. This Web site is dedicated to the belief that the aliens who have been visiting Earth all these years are from a planet orbiting Sirius."

Gilbert laughed nervously. "Well, they've gotta come from somewhere," he joked.

"If there even *is* a 'they'!" David reminded him.

"C'mon, everybody," Joe objected. "We're just getting carried away here. I mean, we've all done enough Web surfing to know that if you're looking for a Web site on something, you can find it . . . no matter how weird the subject might be."

"That's true," Sam agreed. "Just because it's on the Net doesn't mean it's true."

"Uh . . ." Joe interrupted, frowning at the screen. "What was the name of that curly-haired guy Wanda interviewed yesterday at the crash site?"

David looked at him, wondering why he had asked. "You mean the one who was talking about the conspiracy to keep information about UFOs from the public?" He thought about the question until it hit him. "It was Collier, I think. Herbert Collier."

"That's what I thought," Joe said. "Look!"

He was pointing to the name of the author of the "Dog Star" Web page, located at the bottom of the screen.

It was *Professor Herbert Collier!*

Chapter Eight

Seeing that the kids had made good progress on their mystery, Wishbone decided they could spare him for a little while. It was time to check on his friend Sparky.

The Jack Russell terrier left David's house and hurried through the streets of Oakdale. He tried to stay focused on his mission. But, several times on his journey, he ran into one of his two-legged friends. Happy to see Wishbone, they offered him a treat that he couldn't refuse.

"It's a long time until dinner," the terrier reasoned. "Besides, I've had a more than usually active day. A dog on a mission has got to keep up his strength for whatever adventure may come his way next!"

For the second time that day, Wishbone rounded the side of Sparky's owners' house and entered the backyard. He trotted directly to the doghouse. "Okay, Sparky," he called out. "Something's wrong—and you're going to tell me what it is! I won't take 'no' for an answer!"

Slowly, the golden retriever stuck his head out of his doghouse and gazed at Wishbone, barking in greeting.

"Well, that's better," the terrier said. "I've been very worried about you, pal."

Sparky moved his big body out of the doghouse. Then he stood there, wagging his tail.

Wishbone cocked his head, confused. "Sure," he said, "you seem fine now, but you've got to admit you were acting strange the last time I was here. So, you want to tell me what was wrong?"

Sparky sat down on the ground but wouldn't give Wishbone a clue.

At least he's acting more like his old self, Wishbone thought. *And everything* looks *normal. I guess maybe I was just being—*

He stopped short as he looked inside the doghouse. He realized all at once that everything was *not* as normal as he had thought.

"Sparky," Wishbone said, "your new dish—the one with all of those yummy treats in it that you got for your birthday—it's gone!"

Sparky looked away, suddenly unable to meet Wishbone's eyes.

The terrier looked at his friend, horrified. "Who did this terrible thing to you, Sparky?"

As if afraid to answer, the retriever hurried back into his doghouse.

"C'mon, Sparky, old buddy," Wishbone insisted. "You can tell me! Is some bully stealing your stuff again?"

A while back, the good-natured and gentle Sparky had been the victim of a canine bully who had stolen all his favorite toys. Wishbone had helped his pal out then. He had succeeded in getting the bully to leave Sparky alone and return his stuff.

But if a second bully was the cause of the stolen dish—and, worse, the missing food!—the golden retriever seemed too embarrassed to admit it. He wouldn't even let Wishbone come inside his house to sniff around for clues.

After half an hour of trying to get Sparky to tell him what was going on, the terrier was forced to give up. Whatever the problem was, the retriever appeared determined to handle it himself. In the end, Wishbone had to respect his friend's wishes.

"Okay," he told Sparky before he left. "But remember, pal . . . if you change your mind and want some help, I'm always here for you."

Sparky just looked at him.

With a snuffle, Wishbone left the yard, no less worried about his pal than when he had arrived.

As David dialed the telephone in his kitchen, he heard a scratching sound at the door.

Joe smiled. "Sounds like Wishbone," he said. He went to the door. "It's him, all right."

A moment later, the terrier came in and made himself comfortable by the table. Then he looked around, as if he were wondering what he had missed.

"Anybody answering?" Sam asked David.

The boy shook his head. "Not yet," he said. "It's still ringing. I guess there aren't as many people at the college during the summer."

Just then, there was a click. A voice came on at the other end of the line. "Good afternoon," it said. "Oakdale College. How may I help you?"

"Hello," David said. "I was wondering if I could speak to Dr. Marilyn Isaacs. My name's David Barnes. I'm going to be working with her this summer."

"I'm sorry," the operator at the college said. "I'm afraid Dr. Isaacs hasn't returned yet from her vacation."

"Oh," David said, disappointed. "I see."

David had met Dr. Isaacs the year before, while he was checking out Gilbert's hoax. He had brought her the original sample of the object that Wishbone had dug up.

Dr. Isaacs had spent a lot of time with David discussing the mystery of the green glow. She had taken his interest in the phenomenon very seriously. The kids had all hoped she would be available again for further questioning.

Sensing David's disappointment, the operator quickly said, "Perhaps you would like to speak to one of Dr. Isaacs's colleagues instead?"

"That would be great!" David said, his enthusiasm renewed. Smiling, he flashed the others a thumbs-up.

"That would be . . ." said the operator. "Yes . . . there's a visiting professor. His name is Herbert Collier."

David was stunned. "Did . . . did you say Herbert Collier?"

"That's right," the operator told him. "In fact, I see here on the schedule that the professor will be giving a lecture tonight at seven o'clock on one of his favorite topics—UFOs. If you'd like to attend, I'm sure you could speak to him afterward."

"UFOs," David repeated. He couldn't believe how often this man's name kept coming up.

"May I help you with anything else?" the operator asked.

"Oh," said David, jolted back to the reality of the moment. "No. No, thank you. And thanks for all your help, ma'am."

He hung up the phone.

"What did you say about Professor Collier?" Gilbert asked.

David smiled. "You aren't going to believe this . . ." he began.

Chapter Nine

Oakdale College, one of David's favorite places, was located at the north end of town. The small collection of stately brick buildings that made up the campus all faced the College Commons. It was a patch of tree-shaded lawn on which students and teachers alike could relax between classes.

That evening, however, there were only a few students hanging around. After all, even though it was summer, the college ran a full schedule of classes and special lectures. So most students were inside, busy with their course work.

David and the other kids were quite excited by the chance to question Professor Collier. Joe's mom drove everyone to the lecture.

"I've got to admit," she had said, "all this talk of UFO crashes and alien encounters has got me more than a little curious. I wish I could stay, but I'm working at the library tonight. I'll pick you all up after the lecture."

The campus lecture hall was full of both students and local residents. Professor Collier had already begun his talk by the time David and his group of friends arrived.

As quietly as possible, David, Joe, Sam, and Gilbert settled into seats in the back row to listen. Of course, Wishbone came along, as well. He settled himself on the floor next to Joe's chair.

". . . no small coincidence that this very town should be the site of a UFO crash two days before my lecture," Herbert Collier was saying. He was dressed in tan slacks, a blue-denim shirt, and a brown sports jacket. His clothing was so rumpled that he looked as though he had slept in it.

David smiled, figuring that being somewhat messy was all part of being a mad genius. Or maybe it was just part of looking like one.

"Of course," Professor Collier continued, "the official story was finally released this evening. Not a UFO, it said. Oh, no, no. Merely a weather balloon that crashed on a test flight.

"A weather balloon, indeed!" he thundered suddenly. "If that isn't the oldest cover story in the books, I don't know what is. In fact, it dates back to the very first official cover-up back in 1947, at Roswell, New Mexico.

"On or around July 4 of that year, an alien spacecraft crash-landed in the desert. Several days later, the local newspaper, *The Roswell Daily Record,* published a report from an information officer at the Roswell Army Air Field. It stated that a 'flying disk' had been retrieved from a local ranch.

"Well," said Professor Collier, "it seems that the young army information officer acted too quickly. He was punished for his actions, and the air base released different information. Officials there now claimed that what had been retrieved wasn't a flying saucer at all, but rather a group of weather balloons."

He smiled knowingly.

"It didn't matter that many who witnessed the crash, including the rancher on whose property the UFO had come down, claimed that the debris looked nothing like any weather balloon they had ever seen. And ever since that time, 'weather balloons' have been one of the most popular official explanations for UFO sightings the world over."

Professor Collier began to pace in front of his audience. His glasses kept slipping down the bridge of his nose. Each time they did, he impatiently pushed them back up.

"But there have been descriptions of UFOs as far back as 1561 in Nuremberg, Germany. A published report from the time described round red and black objects that appeared to be involved in aerial combat over the city. Surely there can be no claim of weather balloons there," he chuckled.

David couldn't help chuckling along with him. Neither could anyone else in the audience, it seemed.

"And in 1947," said the professor, "a businessman flying his private plane in Washington State reported seeing nine objects flying over Mount Rainier in formation . . . and at speeds of more than sixteen hundred miles per hour! Indeed, from this man's report of the objects moving like saucers skipping across the water came the popular term 'flying saucer.'

"At any rate," he went on, "at first, the U.S. government took UFO sightings seriously enough to classify them as secret. The air force began what was known as Project Blue Book in 1952. Its purpose was to study and investigate all UFO sightings. The project employed a number of scientists, including engineers, meteorologists, physicists, and astronomers.

"The program's goals were threefold," said Collier. "First, to explain all sightings. Second, to learn if UFOs posed a threat to national security. And, third, to see if UFOs were using any advanced technology that might be useful to us humans."

He leaned his elbows on the podium and stared out at his attentive audience.

"And guess what, ladies and gentlemen? By 1969, when Project Blue Book was officially closed down, it had investigated almost thirteen thousand reported UFO sightings and close encounters!

"And yet," said the professor, straightening his glasses on the bridge of his nose, "the government was able to find a way to identify each and every one of those sightings. Every single one was explained away by atmospheric, astronomical, or artificial phenomena, or hoaxes, or dismissed because of a claim of insufficient data."

Professor Collier then went on to discuss the many explanations that had been offered to deny the existence of UFOs. They included not only weather balloons, but satellites, formations of birds, aircraft lights, meteor showers, strange forms of lighting, reflections off windows or eyeglasses, and swamp gas.

"The government does not even accept physical evidence such as radar," said Professor Collier. "That's because they claim so many physical phenomena can give false radar echoes. Rather convenient, isn't it?

"And yet, one must ask: How likely is it that thirteen thousand individual reports over seventeen years could all be wrong? The answer is, of course, that they can't. This can lead us to only one conclusion—the government is covering up the existence of aliens on Earth!"

David shook his head in disagreement. As interesting as Professor Collier's talk was, his conclusion was completely off base. He was claiming that because there was so much evidence something was false, it had to be true.

"Now we come to the famous—or, should I say, disgraceful—Area Fifty-one," Collier continued. "That's the top-secret military base where the remains of the aliens from the Roswell crash have been kept for study. Area Fifty-one also serves as a center for all UFO studies conducted by the government.

"Countless photographs of aliens, their craft, and interviews with people who have encountered alien visitors are on file there. Of course," said the professor, "anyone who has seen an alien is made to believe that he or she has only imagined the encounter. Or else they are accused of being hoaxsters."

"But, Professor," someone called out from the audience, "in all fairness, many sightings *have* been proven to be tricks."

David looked over at Gilbert and smiled to see his friend squirm uncomfortably at the mention of UFO hoaxes.

"Yes, yes," Professor Collier said impatiently. "But just because some people have falsified accounts doesn't mean all accounts are untrue. I myself have seen UFOs. And I have spoken with hundreds of reliable eyewitnesses to other sightings. Why, just the other night in Oakdale, many of your friends and neighbors saw the very spacecraft that crashed on the old Blumenfeld farm. Are they all crazy? Is everyone in your town conspiring to stage a hoax?"

David looked around the lecture hall, taking in the faces of all those attending. Maybe they weren't all part of a conspiracy, but many of them certainly looked willing to accept what the professor was saying.

In some ways, the boy thought, that was the spookiest thing of all.

Chapter Ten

Professor Collier ended his lecture an hour later, after a lengthy question-and-answer session with the audience.

As much as David and his friends were interested in getting Collier to answer their questions, they had decided that it would be best to ask them in private.

Joe pointed out that it wouldn't be wise to let news of their possession of the silver material become known to many people. David and the others agreed.

So after Collier was finished and had made his way through the groupings of people who still wanted to speak to him, the kids stopped him at the rear of the lecture hall.

"Excuse us, sir," David said.

"Yes, young man," Herbert Collier said, blinking at David through the thick lenses of his glasses.

"We met yesterday," David told him, "out by the Blumenfeld farm. We were with Wanda Gilmore."

"Ah, yes. The reporter." Collier smiled. "Well, I'm glad to see this incident has sparked your curiosity about such an important topic."

"Well," David said, "we've actually been interested in UFOs for quite some time now."

"True believers!" the professor declared happily, clapping his hands together.

"Uh . . . not exactly," David said.

"But we *are* curious," Joe added quickly. "I mean, what with the green glow in the sky, the silver material we found not far from the crash site, and the things we saw out at Littleton Aerospace—"

Professor Collier was blinking rapidly. "Silver material, you say? What silver material would this be?"

Joe dug the fragment, now wrapped in an old dust cloth, from his pants pocket. He handed it to Herbert Collier, who took it anxiously and unwrapped it as he frowned deeply.

His eyes widened when he saw what he held in his hand. He scratched it with his fingernail and then bent it between his hands. Without ever taking his eyes off it, he next dug through his jacket pockets until he found a scratched magnifying glass.

Making soft humming sounds under his breath, the professor carefully examined the singed and twisted edges of the material through the glass. Finally, he looked up at the kids.

"Do you have any idea what this is?" Collier asked them breathlessly.

"Gilbert's uncle, Dr. Max Pickering, works at Littleton Aerospace," David said. "He says it's some kind of lightweight, yet strong material that he developed last year."

"Littleton, you say? Max Pickering?" Herbert Collier shook his head and smiled. "I don't think that I know him. However, I'm not surprised that he would say that.

He couldn't possibly tell you that this is of extraterrestrial origin, now, could he?"

"Why wouldn't he, if that's what it really is?" Gilbert said challengingly.

David put his hand on his friend's arm. He could tell Gilbert was tired of hearing his uncle referred to as a liar.

"I've some experience with space-age materials, son," said the professor. "I've never seen a substance even one bit like this one." He turned to Joe. "But tell me about what you saw at Littleton that raised your suspicions."

"It wasn't much, really," the boy said. "Just a star chart with Sirius, the dog star, circled."

"Our guide at the lab," David said, glancing at Gilbert, "tried to pass it off as a harmless joke, but he seemed really nervous when we saw it."

Collier was nodding strongly, thoughtfully stroking

his chin. "Yes, yes. It's widely accepted by UFO experts that Sirius would be a logical home for alien visitors. I believe that myself."

"We know," Gilbert said a little angrily. "We visited your Web site this afternoon."

"And I hope you learned something from it," the professor muttered. But he was still thinking, still fingering the strange piece of material. He eyed David. "I would say from the evidence I've seen that this young man's uncle was lying about the origin of this material."

Gilbert started to object. "That's not true—"

But Collier held up his hand to stop him. "I'm certain your uncle is a good man, but you must understand that Littleton does much of its work for the government and is involved in many top-secret projects. He would have no choice but to . . . let us say, mislead you in certain areas.

"This, for instance," the professor said, holding up the fragment. "It wasn't developed for weather balloons or aeronautic use—at least not of an earthly origin. Rather, I would say, it is a leftover piece of the alien space-craft that crashed on the old farm."

"But how do you know for sure?" David insisted. "I mean, shouldn't you at least analyze the material scientifically and see what it's made of?"

"It's most likely exactly what you were told—a light-weight, yet strong material," said Collier. "Only it's *not* from our planet."

"But if it were from somewhere else," Gilbert cut in, "couldn't we be able to figure that out by examining it under a microscope?"

"Dear boy," Professor Collier chuckled patiently, "the entire universe is made up of the same materials. Silicon from Alpha Centauri or Sirius would be the same as silicon from Earth. Chains of molecules don't change because they're from another planet."

David couldn't believe what he was hearing. "Excuse me, sir," he said, unable to hold back any longer. "I'm not trying to be disrespectful or anything. I'm just trying to understand all of this. It seems to me you haven't offered us any real proof that what you're saying is true."

"It's quite all right, David. You're not being disrespectful," Collier said with a smile. "You are obviously very bright and inquisitive. We wouldn't want to stop that, would we?"

But David knew that the professor hadn't answered his challenge.

Wishbone wasn't sure exactly at what point in the professor's lecture it was when he drifted off to sleep. Somewhere around Roswell, New Mexico, he thought, as he yawned and stretched under the chair where he had settled at the start of the lecture.

He noticed that the seats were all empty. The lecture hall had cleared out, except for Joe, their friends, and the curly-haired man who had been speaking up front.

Lecture's over, is it? he thought. *I . . . wonder if there are any after-lecture snacks being served.*

The terrier wandered over to his group of people. "Still going on about UFOs," he noted. But he observed something else as he came closer to Professor Collier. He sniffed, just to make certain he wasn't mistaken.

No mistake, he thought. *I've never smelled anything like it in my entire life before today. . . . And then I catch a whiff of it twice in the same day!* That odor of fancy soap . . .

It had the same smell as the gum Dr. Pickering had been chewing!

Wishbone circled around Professor Collier and the kids. They were so wrapped up in their conversation that no one took notice of the white-with-brown-and-black-spots terrier.

Whew! Wishbone thought. *That smelly stuff sure gives gum a bad name. Why in the world would anyone want to chew it?*

Then, suddenly, he caught sight of the same red-yellow-and-black plaid packaging he had seen Dr. Pickering pull out of his coat at the lab. It was sticking out of Collier's pants pocket.

Wishbone thought it was strange that two men with such different opinions on the UFO question should happen to chew the same strange gum. *Could my sometimes over-active imagination be playing tricks on me,* he thought, *or is something odd going on here?*

"Anyway," the dog said, "at least the smell's not so bad while it's still in the package. It's certainly not strong enough for a human nose to pick it up. But I bet Joe and the others would want to take note of this strange, odorous coincidence!"

Wishbone paid special attention to the height of the professor's pocket. Fortunately, the professor wasn't too tall. *After all,* Wishbone thought, *even an expert jumper like me has his limits!*

He then backed up a few paces. Next, with a running start, he leaped up at Collier. His snout nudged the package of gum from the man's pocket. It hit the floor with a satisfying little thud.

He shoots . . . and he scores! Wishbone thought triumphantly.

Professor Collier looked down in surprise. "Who do we have here?" he asked.

"This is Wishbone," Joe said, quickly stooping to hold the dog still. "He's with us. I'm sorry, he doesn't usually jump up on people. I guess he just wanted to say hello."

But as Joe released Wishbone and began to stand up, he noticed the package of gum lying on the floor at Collier's feet. He bent down to pick it up.

'Atta boy, Joe! thought the terrier.

"Is this yours?" Joe asked the professor.

Then Joe seemed to recognize the package. Glancing quickly at his friends, he made sure they saw it, too.

"Oh, yes," Collier said, taking the package from him. "It must have fallen from my pocket."

"Ask him where he got it, Joe," Wishbone insisted.

"I don't think that I've ever seen that brand of gum before," Sam said. "Where did you get it, sir?"

Collier shoved the package of gum back into his pocket and shrugged. "Oh, some place in town," he said vaguely. "I don't remember the name. I'm new here, after all." The professor glanced at his wristwatch. "Oh, dear. It's getting late, isn't it? I really must be going."

"Well, thank you for your time," Joe said, shaking his hand. "All your theories are very interesting."

Somewhat hesitantly, Collier handed Joe back the piece of silver material. "Yes, they are. Please, young man," he said to Joe, "if you unearth any more evidence pointing to the existence of UFOs, you must let me know."

"I will, Professor," the boy promised.

After saying good-bye to Collier, the kids and Wishbone left the college's lecture hall. They waited outside for Ellen. David said, "Well, that was weird."

"Definitely," said Sam. "Especially that part with the

gum. I think we'd better check that out first thing tomorrow. I mean, what are the odds that two guys who don't even know each other would be chewing the same odd-smelling gum that we've never even seen before today?"

"Maybe there's some kind of conspiracy going on," Joe said. "Just like in the book I'm reading—Jack London's *The Assassination Bureau.*"

"I don't think I know that story," David told him.

"It's about a man named Dragomiloff. He runs a secret organization that kills people for money," Joe explained. "But Dragomiloff will take a commission to kill someone only after he's determined that the person is unworthy to go on living. For instance, he may decide to get rid of a crooked politician whose cheating ways cause people harm."

"So this Dragomiloff fellow is an honorable murderer?" Gilbert laughed.

"Yes," Joe said. "At least, from his own point of view. But it's more the conspiracy part that I'm talking about. In the book, the conspirators are covering up a ring of murderers. With our situation, it looks like someone's covering up alien visitations to Earth."

"There are no alien visits, Joe!" David insisted.

"Oh, no?" Wishbone said. "Well, that awful chewing gum sure smells like it's from another planet!"

Chapter Eleven

Bright and early Tuesday morning, Wishbone went back to Sparky's house. He had been troubled all night by his friend's strange behavior.

Sparky was usually a very friendly and outgoing dog. For him to act as he had been meant something had to be terribly wrong. If only he would open up to Wishbone, the terrier was sure he could help.

On top of that, Wishbone was worried about Joe's UFO mystery. The kids were on the trail of something important. Most likely, it involved a conspiracy that included Dr. Pickering and Littleton Aerospace. And, from what they had seen at the lecture the night before at the college, maybe Professor Collier was involved in the scheme, as well.

Where would all the clues lead? What did they all mean? Wishbone wished he knew.

"Hey, Sparkster!" the terrier called in the direction of Sparky's doghouse as he entered the backyard.

The golden retriever poked only his head out of the doghouse.

It's as if he doesn't want me to get too close, Wishbone thought. *What's he afraid I'll find out if I do? Maybe he doesn't want me to sniff out whoever it is that's picking on him.*

More and more, Wishbone was becoming convinced that Sparky was once again being bullied by a bigger dog. Maybe this time his pride wasn't letting him seek help, the way he had the last time.

"So," the terrier said pleasantly, stopping in front of the doghouse door. "How's it going today, pal? Thought I'd drop by and see if you were up for a little good, old-fashioned playing."

Sparky just looked at him.

"I couldn't help noticing that you got a new chew toy for your birthday," said Wishbone. "It looked just right for a hearty game of tug-of-war."

Still no response.

But as he talked, the terrier sneaked a look into the doghouse. *That's weird,* he thought. *I don't see the chew toy. First his new dog dish disappears, and now this. It looks as if some thief has taken* both *of Sparky's birthday presents!*

The golden retriever put his chin down on his out-stretched paws.

"Don't feel like playing, huh?" Wishbone said lightly. "You're usually pretty peppy, you know. Are you feeling okay?"

Sparky snuffled.

"Well, all right—if you're sure," the terrier said. "Then I guess I'll just be on my way. But if you decide you want to play . . . or talk . . . or *anything,* you know where to find me, right?"

Sparky blinked sadly at Wishbone. Then he closed his eyes, as if he were going to sleep.

He's not really tired, Wishbone thought. *He just wants to get rid of me—and that's not a good sign! This is one mystery I'm going to have to solve on my own.*

David approached Beck's Grocery on Oak Street with Joe on one side of him and Sam on the other. Their mission was to find out where the strange gum chewed by both Max Pickering and Herbert Collier was purchased. A grocery store was the logical place to begin their search.

But as the kids entered the store and stood before the checkout-counter rack that held all the gum packages, not to mention a variety of candies and mints, they were disappointed. The distinctive red-yellow-and-black plaid package was nowhere to be seen among the many brands of gum.

"It looks like we're out of luck," Joe said in frustration. "Beck's is the only place in town that I can think of that might carry that gum."

"'Morning kids," Mr. Beck said. He was walking toward the trio from the back of the store. "Something I can help you with?"

"Hi, Mr. Beck," David said to the smiling, balding owner of the grocery store. "We were looking for a special kind of chewing gum, but we don't see it here."

"Well," Mr. Beck replied, wiping his hands on the front of his white apron, "I carry most of the popular kinds. What brand, exactly, are you looking for?"

"We don't know the name," Sam told him, "but it comes in a red-yellow-and-black plaid package."

"Oh, that one!" Mr. Beck said, wrinkling his nose in distaste. "It's called Crawley's Chew. I've been special-ordering it for the last couple of weeks for one of my customers. A Mr. Collier—I believe he's a professor of some kind over at the college."

"Is he the only person who buys it?" Sam asked, excited.

"Yep," Mr. Beck said. "Buys it by the box, in fact. I don't bother to put it out on the rack. I tried a piece of it myself. Frankly, I don't think any of my other customers would like it." He made another face. "It's not a taste everyone would enjoy," he said politely. Then he left the kids and went back to continue his chores.

Eureka! David thought. If Professor Collier was the only one ordering the gum, and Gilbert's Uncle Max had some, there was a good chance the two men knew each other! Which meant . . . what?

But what did the chewing-gum connection really prove, even if it existed? Nothing, as far as he could tell.

"What's the matter, David?" Sam asked. She saw the look of puzzlement on her friend's face.

"I'm trying to make sense of all of this," David told her. "Dr. Pickering and Professor Collier share a taste for the same gum. So what? Maybe they really do know each other. Well, again, so what? They're basically in the same line of work, in a way, so it doesn't prove a thing."

"But if they *do* know each other," said Sam, "Professor Collier lied to us. Why would he do that?"

"Boy," Joe said with a sigh. "If this really is some conspiracy, it's a very confusing one."

"Only because we don't have enough pieces of the puzzle," Sam insisted. "We've just got to keep digging for more pieces and hope everything starts to mean something once the other parts of the puzzle fall into place."

"Hey, you two!" Joe said. "Check this out!"

He was pointing to the newspaper rack next to the front door of the grocery store. On it were copies of that day's *Oakdale Chronicle*. The headline read: WEATHER BALLOON CRASHES ON FARM. Below the headline was a copy of the picture of the crash site that Gilbert's uncle had shown them the other day. A smaller headline read: VISITING PROFESSOR CLAIMS UFO COVER-UP. Right next to the title of the front-page article was a boxed notation stating that there was an interview with Professor Collier inside.

Excited, the kids bought a copy of the newspaper. Then they left the store to read the article.

The story, written by Wanda Gilmore, revealed everything that Dr. Pickering had told the kids when they had toured Littleton Aerospace. It said that an experimental weather balloon on a test flight had crash-landed on the Blumenfeld farm.

Because it was a military project, the specifics of what had crashed had been kept top-secret from the public at first. But in order to put to rest people's wild theories and gossip about UFOs, the air force had decided to declassify the information.

Of greater interest to the kids was the interview with Professor Collier, also written by Wanda Gilmore. In it, the professor spoke at length about UFOs and government cover-ups. Most of what he had to say was what they had heard the night before at his lecture.

"Oh, no!" David groaned.

"What?" asked Joe.

"Listen to this," David said, taking the paper. "What the military doesn't know, Professor Collier told this reporter, is that some local young people have recovered a piece of the alien spacecraft from the field near the crash. It's a material completely unknown on Earth."

"He's talking about us!" Joe said excitedly.

"That's right," David confirmed. "And there's more. Professor Collier says Gilbert's uncle claimed to have made a similar piece of material that was discovered last year—and he says *I* was the one who told him that."

Sam seemed stunned. "Professor Collier is just a publicity hound," she said angrily. "He looked at the fragment and quickly decided it was an alien object. He didn't examine it closely or put it through scientific testing. He just wants everyone to believe what he's saying. That way, he can try to prove his theories and make a liar out of Gilbert's uncle and the air force."

David was angry, too. He didn't like the fact that the professor had mentioned his name in the article. It made him feel uncomfortable to be publicly linked to a conspiracy theory.

David was becoming even more determined than before to get to the bottom of the mystery. After all, Max Pickering and Herbert Collier were men of science—and scientists were supposed to reveal the truth, not bury it and make it harder to find!

Wishbone met up with the kids as they walked through town. They were deep in conversation about their mystery and about what they were going to do to solve it.

The terrier would have liked to listen for a while and give the kids a few pointers, as usual. But his problem with Sparky was really bothering him.

"Sorry to interrupt," Wishbone told Joe, pawing at his pal's leg, "but I could really use your help with something."

The brown-haired boy smiled down at Wishbone. "Hi-ya, boy. Where have you been all morning?"

"At Sparky's," the terrier answered. "Something strange is going on with him, but he won't tell me what it is. Maybe he'll listen to you, Joe. Come on!"

Wishbone started to run back in the direction of Sparky's house, but Joe didn't follow. He had gone back to his conversation with David and Sam.

The terrier charged back at Joe, saying, "It'll only take a few minutes." Then he raced off again.

"What's wrong with Wishbone?" David asked.

"It looks as if he wants you to follow him," Sam told Joe.

"Sorry, Wishbone," Joe said, getting down on one knee and scratching the anxious dog behind the ear when he ran back to Joe once more. "I really can't play right now. I promise we'll have a game of catch or something later, though. Okay?"

"This is no time for games," Wishbone said firmly.

But Joe had other things on his mind.

Finally, Wishbone saw that Joe wasn't going to listen to his plea for help. The terrier realized he was really on his own this time. *Well,* he told himself, *one Wishbone is usually more than enough to deal with any emergency!*

With that, he barked a farewell and ran off. This time, he was going to confront Sparky . . . and he wasn't going to let him off the hook until he came up with some answers!

Chapter Twelve

Unfortunately, Sparky was gone by the time Wishbone returned. The yard was empty and the doghouse was deserted.

"I wonder where he's gone off to," the terrier said.

He looked at the doghouse. There was no one home—no one to stop him from conducting a full investigation. "I really shouldn't," Wishbone told himself. "Sparky may not want me sniffing around in there."

But the retriever was obviously in some kind of trouble. He needed his friend's help, even if he would not admit it.

The terrier sat at the entrance to the doghouse for several minutes, debating with himself. "I know that going inside may be against Sparky's wishes," Wishbone said at last, "but I'm not doing it to be nosy! I'm on a mission—it's for his own good!"

His mind made up, Wishbone looked around the yard one last time to make sure Sparky wasn't anywhere nearby. Then he trotted inside, put his sensitive nose to the ground, and began to sniff around.

It all smells perfectly Sparky so far, he thought. *Mmm . . . seems he had some nice liver-flavored snack in here recently. I wish there was some left. All this worrying has made me kind of hungry. . . .*

No, he thought. *Stop that! You've got to concentrate on the job at hand!*

Sure enough, after some more careful investigating, Wishbone detected an odor that definitely did not belong in the doghouse.

"Cat!" he exclaimed in surprise. "There's a definite smell of cat in here." Then he spotted something with his sharp eyes. "And . . . aha! Cat *hairs!* Proof positive of a feline presence!"

It all makes sense now, Wishbone thought sadly as he left the doghouse. *Some sneaky old cat stole Sparky's new dog dish and squeaky toy!* No wonder the poor guy's been too embarrassed to tell me what's going on!

The terrier shuddered. *Being bullied by a cat!* he thought. *How humiliating! But at least now I know what the problem is.*

Having gathered the important information he had been searching for, Wishbone hurried from the yard before Sparky had a chance to return and catch him.

Knowing what the problem is, Wishbone thought positively, *is halfway to figuring out what to do about it!*

Later that day, after lunch, Joe was in his driveway absentmindedly shooting baskets. At the same time, he was reviewing the mysterious events that had happened at the Blumenfeld farm.

Wishbone, who was lying on the lawn with his

muzzle on the ground, wasn't as stirred up as when Joe had seen him in town. In fact, the terrier looked quite thoughtful.

"Care for something to drink?" Ellen asked, walking up to Joe.

Joe smiled. "Sure, Mom."

Ellen went back into the house, and a moment later she came out with a glass of lemonade. "Here you go," she said.

The boy finished off the glass in a few big gulps. Only then did he realize how thirsty he had been. The cold lemonade felt good going down.

"So," said his mother, "have you gotten any further in trying to solve your UFO mystery?"

Joe told her about the chewing-gum coincidence. "But Gilbert's uncle and Professor Collier have such different points of view on UFOs," he went on. "So how *could* they be involved in a conspiracy together?"

"That is a tough question to answer, Joe," his mom said.

Ellen smiled and took the empty glass Joe held out to her. "I'll leave you to your mystery. Let me know how you solve it, all right?"

The boy nodded. "I sure will," he told her, as he watched her go back into the house.

Suddenly, Joe heard his name called from down the street. Turning, he saw David and Sam jogging in his direction. Wishbone had heard them, too, because he stood up and wagged his tail.

"Hi," Joe said, tucking the basketball under his arm and walking over to meet his friends. "What's up?"

"Something," Sam said. Her eyes were bright with excitement as she came up the driveway.

"That's for sure," David added. He held out a piece of paper to Joe. "This was in my mailbox today. Here, take a look."

Joe took the paper and inspected it. It was the torn-off front page of that day's *Oakdale Chronicle*. The black-and-white photograph of the wreckage of the weather balloon was circled in red marker.

Beside it, in the same red marker, were the hand-written words "Check the weather!" and "Balloons don't do this!" Below that it read, "Please keep this letter a secret!" It was signed with the single letter "F."

"What's this all about?" Joe asked, totally confused.

Wishbone barked, as if he wanted to know, too.

"I'm not sure yet," David told him. "But it was in an envelope addressed to me, with no return address. This article just came out this morning, so someone must have just stuck it in my mailbox."

"Someone who calls himself 'F'!" said Sam.

"Wow!" Joe said. Just when he had started to become frustrated about ever solving the mystery, they were handed a new clue—even if they didn't know yet what it meant. "How did this 'F' person know to come to you?"

Before he even finished asking the question, he knew the answer.

"Of course!" Joe exclaimed. "Professor Collier mentioned your name in his interview."

David nodded. "That's right."

Joe looked at the page of the newspaper again and frowned. "What does this mean, exactly?"

"I don't know yet, either," David said, his tone a determined one. "But at least it gives us an idea of what questions to ask next."

"I just wonder who 'F' is," Sam added.

Wishbone leaped up and put his paws on Sam's leg. She knelt and scratched the dog behind his ears.

"I guess Wishbone wonders, too," she chuckled.

"Wow!" Joe said. "The longer this mystery goes on, the more it all reminds me of that guy Dragomiloff in *The Assassination Bureau.* He liked to control people and events from afar—just like this 'F' person is doing now."

"What kind of people?" Sam asked.

"Special agents," Joe told her. "They carried out his plans, which were always moral—at least to Dragomiloff's way of thinking. As far as he was concerned, he was performing a service to humanity by getting rid of evil— even if he had to murder to do it."

"This other character, Winter Hall, thought his actions were questionable," Joe continued. "He finally convinced Dragomiloff that murder, no matter how noble the motive, was never right. So, in order to stay true to his own moral code, Dragomiloff began to destroy the very organization that he had worked so hard to build up.

"The weird thing," said Joe, "is that Dragomiloff

decided the only way to do this was to order his own special agents to assassinate him. Before very long, Hall came to admire Dragomiloff as an honorable but misguided man."

"Whew!" Sam replied, continuing to scratch Wishbone behind his ears. "I wouldn't know who to root for in a story like that."

"I know what you mean," Joe said, holding out the marked-up page from the *Chronicle*. "I feel the same way about our UFO conspiracy!"

Just then, his mom's face appeared through the dining room's open window. "Joe," she said, "Gilbert's on the phone. He says he'd like to speak with you."

The boy went inside and picked up the phone. "Hello?" he said. "Gilbert?"

"Hi, Joe," Gilbert replied. "I just saw today's newspaper. I read that interview with Professor Collier. I can't believe that ridiculous stuff he said about the fragment being from an alien spacecraft."

"Neither can I," Joe said with a shake of his head. "But, listen, something else has come up." He told Gilbert about the torn-off front page that David had received, and he passed on the advice they had gotten from "F."

"That's crazy," Gilbert snapped when Joe was finished. He sounded angry. "Don't tell me you're going to listen to someone who won't even sign a full name!"

"I don't know what to believe anymore," Joe admitted. "But it's clear that somebody is trying to mislead us."

"Believe what you want," Gilbert said. "But if you and Sam and David are really my friends, you'd throw that piece of newspaper away and forget about it!"

With that, Gilbert slammed the phone in Joe's ear.

Joe sighed. Then he went outside to tell his friends what had happened.

"Sounds like Gilbert's angry with us," Sam observed.

"And I'm not sure I blame him," said Joe.

"But we can't dismiss something that might be evidence," David argued. "I mean, I don't want to hurt Gilbert's feelings, either, but I don't like the idea that someone is lying to us . . . no matter who it is."

"David's right," said Sam. "Besides, we've already gotten a pretty good idea that Gilbert's uncle is part of a conspiracy of some kind. It also looks like Professor Collier's involved. Who knows who else could be in on it?"

Joe agreed. "We need to keep searching for the truth," he told his friends. He looked sadly at David and Sam. "I just hope that finding the answer to this mystery doesn't wind up costing us Gilbert's friendship."

"So what do we do now?" asked Sam.

David shrugged. "It seems to me we need to learn about weather balloons . . . and the weather."

Joe nodded. "Sounds good to me. To the Internet?"

His friend smiled at him. "To the Internet!"

While Sam was scratching Wishbone behind his ears, the terrier was thinking about how exciting the kids' mystery was. He wished he could spend all his time helping them solve it.

But Sparky was his closest canine friend. He needed the terrier's help even more than the kids did. Wishbone knew there was only one way for him to get the big retriever out of this fix. It was time for a confrontation!

With that in mind, Wishbone left the driveway with

the kids. However, as they headed for David's place, Wishbone headed toward Sparky's. Quickly, his legs pumping, he made his way across town and raced toward his canine pal's backyard. The closer he got to ground zero, the more determined he became.

No more talking around it, the terrier thought, as he entered Sparky's domain. *I'm going to face off with Sparky and let him know what I sniffed out in his doghouse.*

The retriever might be angry that Wishbone had gone inside without permission. However, he would have to get over that if he ever hoped to solve his problem with that bullying cat!

"It's okay, amigo," Wishbone said, as soon as he saw Sparky standing there in front of his doghouse. "I understand you're embarrassed. I'd feel pretty foolish, too, if some cat was dogging me. But this situation has got to stop! It's not right for anybody, dog or cat, to take what doesn't belong to him. And let's face it, Sparky, it's just not natural for a cat to be picking on a dog!"

Sparky, as usual, said nothing.

"Oh, sure," said Wishbone, "tell me to mind my own business if you want. Still, I can't stand to see my friend in trouble—and so unhappy. Look, if you're worried the other dogs in the neighborhood will find out, you have my word this will stay as our secret."

Sparky turned away.

"C'mon," said the terrier, "this is Wishbone! I'm man's and dog's best friend! Let me help you . . . please!"

But Sparky was firm on the issue. No matter how much Wishbone nagged or pleaded with him, he refused to reveal anything.

"You are one stubborn canine," Wishbone growled.

"The only dog I know who's more stubborn than you is . . . me!"

With that, the terrier turned tail and trotted away. But he wasn't giving up—not by a long shot.

I told him I was stubborn, Wishbone thought. *If that means I've got to stand watch over his yard to catch a bully, then that's just what I'll do. Once I sink my teeth into something, I hold onto it for good—*

"And speaking of sinking my teeth into something," he said, "I could use a little snack break to keep my strength up!"

Chapter Thirteen

Wishbone came trotting into his house through his doggie door. He headed straight for his dog dish. *Ah, lovely,* he thought, seeing that his mid-afternoon snack had already been set out. "But then," he said, "the service here is always excellent!"

After munching on his treats, he looked around and saw that Ellen was the only one home. It didn't take long for a great detective like Wishbone to figure out that Joe and his friends were still at David's house.

"Gotta go," he told Ellen. With that brief farewell, he exited through his door. "After all, the guys are lost without me."

David sighed as he sat in front of his computer monitor and stared at the screen. It seemed he had hit another dead end.

He had believed it would be easy to find information on weather balloons. As it turned out, however, it wasn't.

He had checked three different science Web sites, and none of them had had what he was looking for.

"Trouble?" asked Joe, who was standing beside him.

"Nothing I can't handle," David assured him. "I'll just hook up with another Web site. How's Sam doing?"

Sam turned to him, still holding the portable phone to her ear. "Yes," she said, "that would be great. Thank you very much." Then she hung up.

"Any luck?" David asked her.

"I spoke to the meteorologist's assistant at station WOAK," said Sam. "She said he's out, but he'll call us when he gets back."

David nodded. "Great."

"How about you?" asked Sam.

David shrugged. "It's harder than I thought. It'll just take time."

Suddenly, Joe straightened. "Did either of you hear something?" he asked his friends.

Sam looked at him. "I think I did. It sounded like barking."

Suddenly, they all smiled. "Wishbone!" they said at the same time.

"I'll go downstairs and get him," Joe said.

Taking a deep breath, David tried more Web sites. He concentrated on ones that were linked to popular science magazines. For each site, he called up a list of the articles each magazine had published during the last year.

He found nothing.

"Okay," he said, "let's try the last *two* years."

Joe came into the room with Wishbone trailing behind him. The dog wagged his tail merrily.

"We miss anything?" Joe asked.

"Nothing," said Sam. "Unfortunately."

David frowned. Going back two years hadn't seemed to turn up anything on weather balloons.

Neither did going back three years.

Or four.

David was considering logging on to a different Web site. Suddenly, he saw a reference to something that had been published nearly five years earlier. "Yes!" he called out.

"Have you got something?" asked Sam.

"I think so," David told her.

Opening up the article, he saw that it was long and technical, with a lot of complicated diagrams. Also, it involved some science that David wasn't familiar with. But if it meant learning about weather balloons, he would make his way through it.

Looking at the monitor over David's shoulder, Joe frowned. "I don't think this was written with the average teenager in mind," he said.

"Maybe not," said Sam. "But David's not the average teenager."

Sam had barely finished her sentence when the phone rang. Quickly, she picked it up.

"Hello?" she said. "Yes, that's me. . . . Uh-huh. . . . You can? . . . That's terrific."

David was eager to find out what the WOAK radio meteorologist was telling Sam. But he was also determined to continue his own investigation. He waded through the article slowly, keeping in mind what "F" said about weather balloons not exploding.

Finally, David reached the end of the article. He was still stumped by what their mysterious informant was driving at. Once again, David studied the diagrams that went with the article, hoping to find a clue there.

Then, all at once, it hit him. "I've got it!" he announced. He held his arms up in a little victory celebration and leaned back in his chair.

Sam hung up the phone. "Me, too!" she exclaimed, just as excited as David was.

"What have you got?" Joe asked eagerly. "Come on! Don't keep me in suspense!"

Wishbone cocked his brown-and-black-spotted head, as if he wanted to know, too.

"You first," David told Sam.

"All right," said Sam. "As you know, I asked the weather forecaster at the radio station to check his weather charts for the night the green glow appeared. And guess what! He said the winds were calm that night—not only at ground level, but as high up as three thousand feet."

Joe smiled. "So the wind couldn't have pushed a balloon across the sky very quickly, right? Or caused a balloon to malfunction, the way Dr. Pickering said it did?"

"Right," Sam told him. "That means Dr. Pickering was lying to us." She smiled at David. "Okay, it's your turn."

The boy smiled back at her. "All right. According to the article that I just read, weather balloons do not have engines."

Joe didn't know what to make of that. "So?"

"Don't you see?" asked David, clapping his friend on the back. "If there's no engine, there's no fuel tank. And if there's no fuel tank, the balloon can't explode!"

Joe moved over to David's bed and sat back on it. "So whatever exploded that night was not a weather balloon. It had to be something else!"

"Exactly!" said David.

"And that's what 'F' was trying to tell us?" Joe asked.

"Seems like it to me," David told him.

Wishbone wagged his tail.

"I wonder," said Joe. "Why didn't 'F' just give this information to the newspapers himself?"

"That's something we'll have to ask him," Sam replied. "That is, if we ever meet him."

"I suppose," said David, "he has his reasons for remaining anonymous. But he did do the next-best thing, didn't he?"

"Sending the newspaper clipping to you, you mean?" Joe asked.

David nodded. "He knew from Miss Gilmore's article that we were suspicious about the weather-balloon story. He must have figured we would be eager to figure this out."

"But how do we know whose side 'F' is on?" Joe wanted to know.

David shrugged. "What difference does that make? He led us to the truth."

"So what do we do now?" Sam asked.

"That's a good question," said Joe.

David looked at his friends, giving the matter some thought. "We take what we've got and go to see Miss Gilmore."

Wishbone decided his pals were doing fine in solving their mystery. So he headed back to Sparky's doghouse. His job at the retriever's place wasn't over yet, and he couldn't rest until he had successfully completed his mission.

But this time, he wasn't going to confront Sparky face to face. He had decided to go undercover. He'd stake out the yard to see who was stealing his friend's most precious possessions.

Wishbone settled down behind the fence that separated Sparky's yard from the neighbor's. From there, by peering through some bushes, he had a perfect view of the retriever's doghouse.

Stealth Dog Wishbone reporting for duty, he thought, as he took up the watch. The first thing he noticed was that a brand-new dog dish had been placed at the side of the doghouse entrance. This one was bright red. The terrier couldn't help but notice—and smell—that it was heaped high with a pile of very tempting, crunchy-looking kibble.

His mouth began to water at the sight of the food, but he quickly reminded himself why he was there. "Cut it out, Stealth Dog!" he scolded himself. "There are some things more important than food. Not a lot of them, I'll admit . . . but *some.* And helping Sparky is certainly at the top of the list!"

Sparky had been lying out in the late afternoon sun when Wishbone first arrived. He didn't move, except to change positions, for quite some time.

It was a hot afternoon, and despite the shade of the bushes, Wishbone felt himself growing drowsy. "I hope something happens soon," he said and yawned. "I'd be embarrassed if I fell asleep on the job."

But that didn't happen—because before long, Sparky got to his feet, stretched, and walked over to his dish.

Oh, no! Wishbone thought miserably. *Please, don't start eating. It's bad enough that I've got to look at all that delicious food. . . . I don't think I could stand to watch you while you eat every tempting mouthful of it!"*

As it turned out, the terrier need not have worried. Instead of eating, Sparky took a careful hold of the bowl

with his teeth. Then, with the full bowl of food secured in his mouth, the retriever trotted out of the yard.

Well, that was unexpected, Wishbone thought, as he moved to follow his friend. The terrier kept well back from the other dog. He trailed him at a safe distance and ducked, whenever possible, behind trees, cars, shrubbery, or fences.

But after sleuthing for a couple of blocks, he realized he didn't need to be so careful. Sparky was unaware he was being followed.

And why should he? "When Stealth Dog is on the job," Wishbone chuckled to himself, "the guilty should beware . . . and the innocent have nothing to fear!"

Wishbone didn't have to follow Sparky for long. Three blocks later, the retriever came to a halt before a small Cape Cod–style house with a white picket fence surrounding it. The canine detective surveyed the area carefully. Then he hurried around toward the driveway.

There was a green pickup truck with a load of timber in it parked there. Saw horses were set up in the front yard. The terrier could smell the distinctive and pleasant aroma of freshly sawn wood in the area.

He could hear men's voices inside the house over sounds of hammering and the harsh whine of a power saw. *Obviously,* Wishbone thought, *this house is undergoing renovations. What reason can Sparky possibly have for bringing dog food here?*

"Well," he said, "there's only one way to find out." With that mission in mind, he started up the walk to the front door.

Before he could get very far, however, a man wearing jeans, a T-shirt, and with a tool belt around his waist appeared in the doorway.

"Hi-ya, fella," the man said to Wishbone. "You want to come in here? I don't think that's such a good idea. It's pretty dangerous for a little guy like you."

"Who are you calling 'little'?" Wishbone shot back, leaping up on his hind legs. "Besides, I'm perfectly willing to wear a hard hat if that will help."

The man laughed and waved his hands at Wishbone. "Off you go, boy. Go on, get home now before your people start to worry about you."

"My people have absolute faith in my ability to take care of myself, thank you very much," Wishbone said, insulted. But he saw he wasn't going to make it past the man into the house.

He decided to retrace his steps. He crossed the street and took up a position behind a tree. From there, he watched for Sparky.

He didn't have to wait long. A minute later, a different workman led the golden retriever out the door by his collar.

"Must be a dog convention in the neighborhood," the first man said with a laugh to the second.

Sparky didn't seem to mind, however. His tail wagging,

his tongue lolling happily in his mouth, the retriever trotted away from the house and headed back toward his home.

Wishbone noticed that Sparky no longer had his dish. He had left it in the house!

Well, I guess this hasn't been a total waste of time, Wishbone decided. *At least I know where Sparky's belongings have been going. Now all I've got to do is wait until the workers go home for the day to get inside—and find out why!*

Satisfied that Sparky's secret was within his grasp, Wishbone headed back to his own house.

Chapter Fourteen

Wishbone sat in Wanda's kitchen, along with Joe, David, and Sam. The terrier looked closely at Wanda's face.

The woman's eyes were wide with excitement. After all, David had just finished telling her what he and his friends had discovered earlier that afternoon about the differences between Dr. Pickering's statements and what they had learned about weather balloons.

Wanda scribbled notes feverishly. "That's amazing!" she told David.

"But, please," Joe insisted, "double-check with an expert. Information on the Internet is not always accurate. This is too important for us not to be absolutely positive!"

"I know a professor of meteorology I can call," Wanda said. "He can confirm what you are saying about the weather. Thank you for supplying me with all this information," said Wanda. She looked at each of the kids in turn. "All of you. This is going to make everyone sit up and take notice! One last thing I need to know, though . . ."

"I told you everything we found out," David said.

"Except the name of the person who told you to question the explosion," Wanda noted. Her pencil was poised over her pad, ready to write down the name.

Wishbone shook his tail, remembering what "F" had said.

David looked at his friends and sighed. "Sorry, Miss Gilmore, but our source asked us not to bring him into this."

Wanda was disappointed. "Then how can we be sure he knows what he's talking about?"

Joe shrugged. "If your expert confirms David's suspicions, then I'd say he knows what he's talking about."

"Well said," Wishbone told the boy.

Wanda nodded. "All right, then. We'll do it your way."

"Great!" said Wishbone. "Let's get those printing presses rolling! We've got a paper to get out! News to spread!"

David knocked eagerly on Joe's kitchen door, a copy of Wednesday's *Oakdale Chronicle* tucked under his arm.

When Joe answered, David stuck the morning newspaper in front of him. He held it there so his friend could read the headline.

"'Doubt Cast on Littleton's Weather Balloon Story,'" said Joe. He smiled. "That's great!"

David pointed to the article below. "Check this out," he said, reading from it: "'A meteorologist, Professor Warren Kaye, of Milford University, agreed that the story of a crashed weather balloon caused by an explosion seemed doubtful. "Weather balloons don't shoot across the sky," said the professor, "and they don't explode under any circumstances. I'm afraid someone has been misinforming people, though I can't imagine why."'"

David looked up at Joe, and both boys grinned. Then they high-fived each other.

Wishbone seemed happy, too. He got on his hind legs and wagged his tail.

"There's more," David said. He read on: "'A spokesperson for Littleton Aerospace, the company that built the weather balloon, responded to these charges. "Professor Kaye's analysis is based on rumor," Dr. Pickering said. "I don't think it really means anything."'"

"Wow!" said Joe. "Gilbert's uncle didn't even try to address the charges."

"Because he can't," David said. "Now maybe some other people will start looking into this matter and we can finally get to the bottom of it."

"I sure hope so," Joe said. "Trying to figure it out is starting to give me a headache."

"Hey, Joe!" came another voice.

David turned and looked out the open kitchen window. He saw Gilbert Pickering.

"Hi, David," Gilbert said. "Hi, Joe." He shrugged. "Is it okay if I come in?"

"Sure," Joe replied. Gilbert walked into the kitchen. "You know you're always welcome here," he told Gilbert.

Wishbone barked, as if in agreement.

"I wasn't sure," Gilbert said, "after the way I hung up on you yesterday." He looked very serious. "Sorry about that. I guess I was just having a problem with the way everybody was talking about my uncle."

"It's all right," Joe assured him. "We understand."

Gilbert noticed that David had a *Chronicle* in his hand. "I see you guys have already read the story, huh?"

Joe fidgeted uncomfortably. "Actually, Gilbert," he said, "we were the ones who gave the story to Miss Gilmore."

Gilbert nodded. "I figured that. And I was angry when I started to read it, but then I read Uncle Max's response. . . ." He paused and took a deep breath. "It didn't sound very convincing, did it?"

David shook his head. "Not . . . really . . ." he said slowly. He saw Wishbone come over and sit down beside him.

"I didn't think so, either," Gilbert said sadly. "So I called him and asked him what was going on. He said he couldn't talk about it over the phone. But he invited us to go back out to Littleton this morning. He said he's explain everything then."

Joe smiled. "That's great."

"If," Gilbert said pointedly, "he actually *does* tell us the truth this time!"

Joe clapped the blond boy on the shoulder. "Come on, Gilbert. Have some faith. Besides, now that we know what crashed was not a weather balloon, what could your uncle have left to mislead us about?"

David grunted as he knelt down and petted Wishbone. "That's a good question," he said, still suspicious.

Wishbone walked back and forth across the hard floor in Dr. Pickering's office. "All right," the annoyed canine said, "let's hear it. And this time, make it the truth, please!"

Joe, David, Sam, and Gilbert no doubt wanted to hear the same thing. However, it seemed they were more patient.

The scientist cleared his throat. He was more quiet than he had been the last time they had visited. The terrier figured that was because the man was a little embarrassed. After all, he had been caught in a lie both by the *Chronicle* and by his nephew.

Finally, Dr. Pickering spoke up. "First of all," he said, "I want to apologize for misleading you all the other day." He looked directly at his nephew. "Especially you, Gilbert. You know that I never would have lied to you if it wasn't a matter of importance and security."

Gilbert smiled. "I figured it had to be something like that, Uncle Max."

"The project I've been working on was classified top-secret by the military," Dr. Pickering continued. "It's something we call . . . Project Sirius."

Wishbone's ears perked up and he began to wag his tail. "Now we're getting somewhere!" he said.

"You mean like Sirius, the dog star?" Sam asked.

Max nodded. "That's right. It's the brightest star in the sky, and one of the closest to our own sun."

"So that's why Sirius was circled on that star chart in the lab next door!" Joe exclaimed.

"Exactly," Max said. "The project is also linked to that fragment of material you found near the crash site. You see, Project Sirius doesn't involve a weather balloon, as we've been telling everybody."

"Then what is it all about?" David asked.

"It's a . . . flying saucer," Max Pickering announced dramatically.

"Get outta town!" said Wishbone, leaping back a step.

Chapter Fifteen

David could only stare at Max Pickering in shock. A flying saucer! The boy hadn't believed that UFOs were of extraterrestrial origin. So he never expected a scientist like Max to come out and say that they were.

"Then," David said with a disbelieving shake of his head, "there really *are* flying saucers and beings from outer space that have come to Earth?"

Wishbone wagged his tail, as if he were expecting an answer, too.

"What?" Dr. Pickering blinked at him in confusion for a moment. Then a big, embarrassed smile spread across his face. "No, I'm sorry. I didn't mean an *alien* flying saucer. I'm referring to one that we have been trying to design and build here at Littleton for some time now."

David found that he had been holding his breath. He forced himself to exhale.

While relieved to hear that there hadn't actually been strange creatures from another planet flying around Earth, he was also a little disappointed. *Imagine the adventures that would have been possible if aliens were here!* David thought for a moment.

"The aim of Project Sirius has been to develop a saucer-shaped reconnaissance craft for the military," Max said.

"You mean, like a spy plane?" Gilbert asked.

"Well . . . yes," his uncle answered. "The saucer shape offers greater possibilities of secrecy capabilities. The right design, using the right materials, would make such a craft almost invisible to radar. A small, remotely controlled ship would have many uses in military situations.

"So far, however," he continued, "we've only built a prototype—a model. Unfortunately, that is what crashed out on the old farm. Let me show you what it looked like."

With that, he went over to a drawer in one of the workbenches and took out a drawing of the craft. It showed a flying-saucer-shaped ship that had some kind of a propeller in its middle. David and the other kids passed it around.

"It's a shame," said Gilbert's uncle. "The prototype was very fast and easy to maneuver. One of the most exciting things about it was that it was powered by hydrogen."

"Hydrogen?" David echoed.

"That's right," said Dr. Pickering. "It's an experimental fuel that might one day power everything from cars to planes."

Sam said, "Not that we're not glad to finally get some answers, Dr. Pickering . . . but why are you telling us all this now?"

"Well," said the scientist, "just yesterday we got word from the military. Due to all the publicity and the loss of the only prototype, Project Sirius has been declassified—it's no longer a secret operation. Everybody feels that it's more important to set the public's minds at ease about the crash than worry about security for a program that may never go beyond the drawing board."

Joe nodded. "So the silver material . . . ?"

"Definitely made here on Earth," Max said with a chuckle. "Developed right here in this very laboratory, in fact. Then it was used in the saucer. We'll be holding a press conference later today to tell everybody what was going on."

The kids exchanged looks. Wishbone cocked his head, as if he knew exactly what was going on.

"I guess that answers everything," Gilbert said. "Thanks for telling us the truth, Uncle Max."

Max playfully ruffled his nephew's hair. "I'm just sorry I had to lie to all of you," he apologized. "But the nature of my work, my security clearance . . . Well, I hope you understand that I didn't really have any choice." He laughed. "I would have had to lie to my own mother about the work I was doing here."

"Grandma would have been able to tell," Gilbert warned with a laugh. "You never would have gotten away with it."

"I wasn't successful in hiding the truth from all of you, either," Max Pickering pointed out.

David acknowledged the statement with some pride. Gilbert's uncle had tried to cover up the truth—but the kids had uncovered it again. To David's way of thinking, he and his friends had a lot to be proud of.

Later that day, Joe and his friends David and Gilbert were relaxing with Wishbone on the steps of Joe's front porch after a hard game of one-on-one basketball.

They realized that they had spent the last few days digging into the mystery of the green glow and finding answers to the Sirian Conspiracy, as Joe had jokingly named it.

While they were relieved to have answers at last, they agreed that all this work was no way to spend their summer vacation. They owed themselves some rest and relaxation, which was what brought them to the hoop in Joe's driveway.

For dinner, they planned to meet Sam at Pepper Pete's Pizza Parlor. She had gone there to help her father with the lunch rush. For the time being, though, the boys were just enjoying the feel of the breeze on their sweaty faces.

"I still can't believe we really saw a flying saucer," Joe said, stroking Wishbone's fur.

"Me either," Gilbert chimed in. "And it's even harder to believe it when I think that my uncle helped build it!"

"I wonder . . ." David said thoughtfully.

Gilbert looked at him. "Hey," he said, "I think that we've had enough conspiracies to last us a while without creating more."

David smiled. "Okay, okay," he said. "But there are still a few questions that we never did get answers to."

"Like what?" Gilbert asked.

"Well," David said, "first of all, we still don't know if there's a connection between your uncle and Professor Collier. Remember, they both chew that same strange gum."

Wishbone snuffled, as if he didn't want to think about the foul-smelling gum.

"Maybe it's just a coincidence," Joe suggested.

"Maybe," David said skeptically. He looked at Gilbert, who just shrugged.

"I don't know," said Gilbert. "I don't remember ever seeing Uncle Max chew that stuff before the other day. And believe me, I would have remembered something that smells that bad."

"And how about our mysterious informant—'F'?" Joe added. "We still don't have a clue as to who he is or how he is involved."

Gilbert groaned. "I thought we have retired from conspiracy-busting."

"Well, we can't just drop the matter without having all the answers," David said. "I don't know about you guys, but I need to have all the loose ends tied up nice and neat before I can let this go."

Wishbone stood up and wagged his tail, as if he agreed.

Gilbert groaned and flopped onto his back. "You're right," he said with a sigh.

Joe said, "This is more and more like the book I'm reading, *The Assassination Bureau*."

"In what way?" David asked.

"Well," said Joe, "even after Dragomiloff agrees to close down the Bureau and puts Winter Hall in charge of the final assassination—that of Dragomiloff himself—Dragomiloff is still in control. He keeps everybody off balance in order to maintain control."

"I see what you mean," said David. "You feel that 'F' is doing the same thing with us. He sits back, sends out a message, and makes us do all the work!"

"We don't have to do what he wants," Gilbert pointed out.

Joe shrugged as Wishbone wagged his tail again. "In

the book, Winter Hall doesn't want to do what Dragomiloff wants him to do, either. All Hall wants to do is shut down the Bureau. But Dragomiloff insists that the only way to do that is to destroy him—the man who created the Bureau in the first place. And since Hall is the one who has convinced Dragomiloff that this is the right thing to do, he winds up with no choice but to try to arrange Dragomiloff's death."

"So," said David, "you think 'F' was counting on the fact that we would want to do the right thing—just the way Dragomiloff has counted on Winter Hall to do the right thing."

Joe nodded. "Something like that. I am still trying to work out all the details."

"But we also believed the truth should come out," David said. "So did we help this mysterious 'F,' or did 'F' help us?"

"David's got an excellent point," Gilbert said. "How do we know if we were puppets or partners?"

"I wish I knew," Joe said thoughtfully.

Chapter Sixteen

On Thursday morning, David's mom was out shopping. He was alone in the house, thinking about the unresolved parts of the mystery and sighing.

When Dr. Pickering had admitted that he had lied to the kids, David had felt relieved. But now he felt dissatisfied. He didn't like the idea that some questions might remain unanswered.

Maybe I'll go over to Joe's, he thought. Then he heard the rustle of the mail carrier placing the Barnes's mail in their mailbox.

David walked to the door, opened it, and took the mail out of the box. To his surprise, there was a letter there without a return address.

It must be another letter from "F"! David could just feel it in his bones. Tearing the envelope open, he took a look inside.

But there was no newspaper clipping inside this time. In fact, the boy realized, there was no message at all—at least not like before. There was just a piece of paper with a word on it. It seemed to David that it was in the same handwriting "F" had used last time. However, the only clue was one word. . . .

Forbidden.

He made a face, then looked at the word again. *Forbidden?* What kind of a clue was that? What was "F" trying to tell him and his friends?

David called Sam and asked her to meet him at Joe's house. Maybe Joe and Sam could help him figure it out.

Joe looked at the letter that had come from "F." "'Forbidden'?" he read out loud. "What's that supposed to mean?"

David shrugged. "I was hoping *you* might know."

"Let me see that," said Sam.

Joe gave her the letter and watched her read it. Sam's forehead wrinkled as it always did when she was concentrating hard on something. Finally, her mouth pulled up at the corners and she smiled.

"What is it?" asked David.

Joe looked at Sam. "Do you know what 'F' is trying to tell us?"

His friend nodded. "I think maybe I do."

"Well, don't keep it to yourself!" David told her.

"It's another clue," Sam told him. She looked at Joe. "But it's not about the crash site or weather balloons or anything like that."

Then what *is* it about?" asked David.

Sam headed for the front door. "Come on," she told the boys. "Follow me and I'll show you."

As she went outside, Joe looked at David. His pal shrugged to show he had no idea what their friend was up to. Joe shrugged back at him just as puzzled. Then the two of them left the house and hurried after Samantha. Wishbone trailed along after them.

Just as Joe and David were doing, Wishbone followed Sam for a while. He was curious to know where she was going. She led them on a winding path across town, to a section the terrier had visited the day before.

"Hey," he told himself, "this isn't far from the house Sparky disappeared into—and got put out of."

In fact, it was only a couple of blocks away from the place. Maybe there wouldn't be any workers around to shoo Wishbone away.

The terrier didn't want to leave Joe and his friends even for a minute. However, he was sure he could investigate the renovated house and find the kids again before they had gone much farther.

Smelling an opportunity, Wishbone glanced at Joe and his friends. "See ya later," he told them apologetically. "Duty calls."

Letting the kids go their own way, the terrier trotted quickly down one street and then the next. He located the house with the white fence around it.

As he had hoped, there weren't any workers around. Wishbone took advantage of that fact. He slipped through the hole in the fence, crossed the front yard, and took a closer look at the house.

The door was locked, of course. But Wishbone saw another way in—through a glassless opening in the frame of a basement window. He poked his nose in first—*always a wise choice,* he thought.

It was dark down in the basement, even in the middle of the day. But the terrier's ears were sharp enough to hear something rustling in the shadows. And his nose told him what it was.

A cat! he realized. *It's a loafing feline!*

Wishbone congratulated himself on his superior detective skills. Stealth Dog had been right about a cat being involved in the mystery surrounding Sparky. But he still didn't understand what had made his canine pal travel all the way across town to give a feline his prized possessions.

It's one thing to give in to a bully when the bully comes to you, the terrier thought. *But saving the bully the trip . . . well, that's just a bit too much, even for a gentle dog like Sparky.*

Wishbone slipped through the hole in the window. He leaped down to the basement floor. The bottoms of his paws were cold from the cement floor, and his eyes were adjusting to the darkness.

But he wasn't nervous. No matter how big or tough the cat was, he was going to stand up to it. After all, he wasn't some easygoing golden retriever whom any wild cat could push around. He was the kind of dog who stood up for his rights—and for his friends' rights, too, when it was necessary.

Padding closer to the rustling sound, Wishbone sniffed the air again. The scent of cat was getting stronger. However, he still didn't see anything feline moving around.

Then he realized where both the sound and the scent were coming from—an old red-flannel blanket in a corner of the basement. And Sparky's bowls and his chew toy were sitting alongside it.

Moving even closer, the terrier peeked into the folds of the blanket. A tiny mewing sound came out of it. A moment later, it was followed by a little black cat's head, its green eyes blinking uncertainly at him.

Gosh! thought Wishbone. *It wasn't a full-grown cat Sparky has been coming to see there. It's just a baby—a kitten.*

Then another head poked out from the blanket. It was just as black as the first. Then a third head appeared, except this one was mostly orange, with some black streaks.

Not one kitten, thought Wishbone, but *three.*

He looked around. There was no sign of the kittens' mother. As far as he could see, they were all alone in the world.

"No," he realized with a start. "Not *all* alone. You had Sparky to help you, didn't you?" All of a sudden, the whole situation became clear to the terrier.

His friend Sparky hadn't gone to the basement to

give his things away to a bully. He had gone to give the helpless kittens something to eat and a toy to play with.

With trust in their eyes, the kittens climbed out of their blanket one by one. Two of them stuck their faces in one of Sparky's bowls to nibble at some food. The third one stretched itself and nudged the retriever's chew toy with its little nose.

Suddenly, Wishbone heard a noise at the window. His fur stood up straight as he went into high alert. He whirled around and saw something big moving around outside—something with orangelike fur and a long snout.

The terrier relaxed. He would know that fur and that snout anywhere. As he watched, his friend Sparky squeezed through the hole in the window and leaped down to the basement floor. Only then did the big dog realize that Wishbone was standing there waiting for him.

Sparky looked at the terrier, then looked at the kittens. Then he looked at the terrier again. Obviously, he was a little confused. It was more than a bit unusual for a dog to be taking care of a litter of cats.

Normally, Wishbone wouldn't have given a feline the time of day. However, the kittens were too small to be any trouble. And Wishbone had to admit they were kind of cute. Besides, they were helpless.

Under the circumstances, he had to admit that he was proud of his buddy the golden retriever. Wishbone began to wag his tail.

"You know what?" he told Sparky. "You're all right, pal."

His friend didn't answer, of course. But then, that was Sparky. He let his actions do the talking for him.

Chapter Seventeen

Thanks to his fine-tuned nose, Wishbone was able to leave the basement and catch up with Joe and his friends in almost no time at all. The kids were standing at a corner by a street sign.

"Here we are," he heard Sam say.

Joe looked around. "I don't understand. All I see are houses."

"Me, too," said David. "What's that got to do with 'Forbidden'?"

Sam hooked a thumb over her shoulder. "What does that street sign say?" she asked her friends.

Joe looked up. So did David. As the terrier watched, a sense of understanding seemed to dawn in the boys' expressions. "What?" he asked, hopping up onto his hind legs.

"Oh, yeah!" said David. "I get it now!"

"Me, too!" Joe exclaimed. He hit his forehead with the palm of his hand. "'Forbidden'—it's an address. *Number four Bidden Avenue!*"

Sam smiled. "Pretty clever of our friend, huh?"

"Pretty clever of *you!*" said Joe. "I don't know if I could have figured that out myself."

"All right, already," said Wishbone. "That's enough patting on the back. Let's get down to business."

David looked around and then pointed. "It looks like the numbers on the houses are going down in this direction. And there's number twelve."

The kids started to walk down the block. Naturally, Wishbone was right at their heels, wagging his tail with anticipation.

"Number ten," said Joe. "Number eight."

"It's up there," David announced, pointing again. "See over there? Number four."

As they neared the house, the kids slowed down. Four Bidden Avenue was a small, dark wooden house. Big pine trees blocked the windows on both sides of the front door.

Joe took a deep breath, then let it out. "I guess this is it," he said.

David swallowed as he gazed at the house. "I guess . . ."

"Come on," said Sam. "Let's do what we came here for."

"Yeah," said Wishbone. "We're not getting any younger, you know."

With Sam in the lead, they followed a brick walk up to the front door. Joe was the one who found the doorbell first. He pressed it.

Wishbone heard a ringing inside the house, followed by the sound of approaching footsteps. Then the door swung open to reveal a man with pale blond hair and bushy eyebrows.

The terrier had seen the man before. But where?

Suddenly, he remembered. The man had been at the old farm the morning after the crash!

"Er . . . we don't mean to bother you," Sam said awkwardly, "but we got a—"

"A note?" the man suggested. He smiled a grand-fatherly smile. "Actually, two notes. And the second one said one word, 'Forbidden.'"

Sam smiled back. "That's right."

The man pointed to a path that ran along the side of the house. "Why don't you kids head around to the back-yard? I'll whip up some lemonade and we can sit down and have a chat." He looked at Wishbone. "And as for you . . . I think I've got a couple of juicy spare ribs left over from dinner last night. Maybe I can dig up a few of those, as well."

"Mighty neighborly of you," Wishbone said.

As the man went back inside the house, the terrier followed his friends into the backyard.

There was a round picnic table with four benches there. Joe, Sam, and David each sat down on one of them. Wishbone found a butterfly to chase.

After a few minutes, the man with the busy eyebrows came out the back door with a tray. It held a big pitcher of lemonade, four tall glasses, and a plateful of spare ribs.

Wishbone's mouth began to water. After all, he hadn't eaten in more than an hour.

"Thanks," said each of the kids as the man poured the lemonade for them.

"Yeah, thanks," said Wishbone, watching the man set the plate of spare ribs down on the ground.

"Don't mention it," their host told them. Then he poured a glass for himself, as well, and sat down on the fourth bench.

Joe sipped from his glass of lemonade. Then he turned to the man with the bushy brows. "My name's Joe Talbot." He tilted his head toward David. "And this is David Barnes." Then he tilted his head again. "And this is Samantha Kepler."

The man smiled. "I read your names in the local newspaper, but it's good to be able to match them up with your faces." He glanced at Wishbone. "And who's this, if I may ask?"

You certainly may, thought the terrier, digging into a beefy spare rib. *You can ask me anything, any number of times—just keep the snacks a-coming!*

"That's Wishbone," Joe replied.

"Nice to meet you all," said their host. "My name is Martin Krantz." He looked around the table. "I bet you're all pretty curious about me."

David nodded. "We sure are."

Mr. Krantz's eyes seemed to lock on something far away. "It all started thirty-two years ago," he said. "In those days, I was an engineer with Littleton Aerospace— the same Littleton Aerospace that tried to pull the wool over your eyes."

Interesting, thought Wishbone, as he continued to gnaw at his spare ribs.

"I was in charge of developing a special kind of aircraft for the company called a military reconnaissance plane. That meant it was supposed to fly out over enemy territory and gather information on what the enemy was doing."

Mr. Krantz sighed.

"It was a different world back then," he continued. "Countries had recently gone to war with one another. They didn't trust their neighbors, so they spied on them.

"But after a while, I found I didn't like the idea of designing aircraft that would be used to spy on other countries. The more I thought about it, the less I wanted to be a part of the spy game. So I quit my job and found something else to do with my life. I took a position as a clerk in Oakdale's Town Hall. I've been there for more than a quarter of a century now."

Mr. Krantz took another sip of his drink.

"But why," he asked himself, "am I telling you all this? That's what you want to know, right?"

"Yes, sir," said Sam.

"The question *had* crossed my mind," Wishbone added.

"Well," Mr. Krantz told them, "I still feel the way I felt thirty-two years ago—I don't want to be associated with Littleton Aerospace or any of its work. That's why I couldn't send my note to the newspaper—even without signing it. The *Chronicle* or some other paper might have found a way to trace it to me.

"On the other hand," he said, "I didn't want Littleton Aerospace to get away with its cover-up. In other words, I needed a way to expose what the company was saying without exposing myself, as well."

David nodded, looking as if he understood. "And that's where we came in."

"Exactly," the man with the bushy brows replied. "When I saw you kids mentioned in the *Chronicle* article, I saw my chance to expose the weather-balloon cover story through *you*."

"But how do you know you can trust us?" Sam asked Mr. Krantz. "With your identity, I mean."

He smiled. "You proved you could be trusted when you gave the information to the *Chronicle* and didn't identify where you had gotten it. Then you proved your cleverness by deciphering the clue I gave you and finding where I live."

"You know," said Joe, "you're a lot like Dragomiloff, the man who's behind The Assassination Bureau in Jack London's book."

"I am?" asked Mr. Krantz.

The boy nodded. "You worked on something, decided it was wrong, and then you got out of it. And just like Dragomiloff, you worked behind the scenes, guiding us to other people instead of acting on your own."

The man chuckled. "I have to confess that I haven't read *The Assassination Bureau,* but this Dragomiloff sounds like my kind of man."

"I guess Herbert Collier was wrong, then," David observed. "He said an alien spaceship crashed at the Blumenfeld farm."

Mr. Krantz shook his head. "I wouldn't put too much stock in what Herbert Collier says. I've learned through the Internet that he's putting out a book on unidentified flying objects. I think all Collier's spouting off is just a way to promote the sales of that book."

"You found that on the Internet?" Sam asked. She sounded surprised.

"Sure did," the man told her. "I got out of the aerospace field, but I try to keep up on things through the Internet, science magazines, and the newspapers."

"Well," said David, looking at Joe, then at Sam, "I guess that pretty much answers all our questions. Thanks for spending the time explaining things to us, Mr. Krantz."

"It was my pleasure," the man with the bushy brows told him.

Then he reached into his pants pocket and took something out.

Wishbone's eyes widened as he saw what it was—a red-black-and-yellow plaid package of gum. From its unpleasant scent, Wishbone could tell it was the same brand Gilbert's uncle and Herbert Collier liked to chew.

Mr. Krantz held the unusual package out to Sam, David, and Joe. "Any of you care for some gum?" he asked cheerfully.

The kids all stared at the gum as if it were a three-eyed alien.

"Er . . . no, thanks," David said with a gulp.

"Me, either," said Joe, holding his hand up.

"Thanks, anyway," Sam muttered.

"I guess we'll be going now," said David.

"Yeah," Joe chimed in, still gaping at the package of gum. "Going."

With that, the kids got up from the picnic table and made their way out of Mr. Krantz's yard. Wishbone trotted out along with his friends—not that he wanted to leave those delicious spare rib bones behind, but the smell of that gum had given him the creeps.

It was only after the terrier and his friends were in front of the house and out on the sidewalk again that they dared to look at one another. Their mouths were hanging wide open.

Finally, it was David who broke the silence. "If we were right about people who chew that gum being involved in a conspiracy—"

"Then Mr. Krantz is in cahoots with Gilbert's uncle and Professor Collier," Joe said, picking up his pal's train of thought.

"And everything he told us could be *dis*information,"

David concluded. He wrinkled his nose. "And maybe aliens *did* crash at the old farm."

Sam shook her head. "No. That can't be," she insisted. She looked back at Mr. Krantz's house and asked in a small voice, "Can it . . . ?"

Wishbone looked up at the sky. Somewhere up there, out in space, was the dog star Sirius. Was it possible there really *were* aliens up there? And had they visited Earth after all?

For once, the fearless terrier wasn't sure he wanted to know.

Suddenly, he remembered a piece of business he had left unfinished here on Earth.

"Come on, Joe," Wishbone told his pal. "I need to show you what Sparky has been up to. Maybe you know someone who'd like a stray kitten."

About Michael Jan Friedman

Michael Jan Friedman is a *New York Times* best-selling author. He has written or cowritten nearly forty science fiction, fantasy, and young-adult novels. More than 5 million of his books are currently in print in the United States alone.

As a lifelong science fiction fan, it was a pleasure for Michael to cowrite *The Sirian Conspiracy* with his friend Paul Kupperberg. Like Wishbone and his friends, Michael liked to stare at the stars as a child and wonder what might be up there. In fact, he still does.

He thinks the only thing better than watching the stars twinkle in the vastness of space is watching them twinkle in the eyes of his children. But then, as he's come to learn, the greatest adventures—and the greatest mysteries—are the ones we find in one another.

Michael became a freelance writer in 1985, after the publication of his first novel, *The Hammer and The Horn*. Since then, he has written for television, radio, magazines, and comic books, though his first love is still the novel.

A native New Yorker, he lives with his wife and two sons on Long Island, where he spends his free time (what there is of it) sailing on Long Island Sound, jogging, and following the adventures of his favorite team, the New York Yankees.

About Paul Kupperberg

Paul Kupperberg is a freelance writer and full-time editor who has worked in the comic-book industry since 1975. As an editor, he has helped to shape the adventures of some of the world's best-known superheroes with some of the most talented people in the business. As a writer, Paul has penned more than 700 stories, some of them about superhero, adventure, and fantasy characters of his own creation.

He has also written two superhero adventure novels (*Murdermoon* and *Crime Campaign*), magazine articles, movie parodies, and syndicated newspaper comic strips. He recently had a piece of fiction published on the Internet, a first for a writer who loves the printed word and the feel of a book in his hands.

The Sirian Conspiracy is Paul's first WISHBONE Mysteries title, although he hopes it's not his last. He has always been a big fan of mystery stories, and he reads as many as he can, especially the ones with the hard-boiled, tough-guy school of detectives. *The Sirian Conspiracy* was especially fun to write because it combined three of Paul's favorite topics: mystery, the writing of Jack London, and outer space.

As a youngster, Paul was an avid follower of the space program. He remembers watching the early *Mercury*, *Gemini*, and *Apollo* missions on TV. The day astronauts Neil Armstrong and Buzz Aldrin made the first lunar landing and walked on the moon remains one of Paul's most thrilling memories. Even today, watching the space shuttle blast off on a pillar of fire gives him great, big goose bumps.

If aliens are watching us, Paul says hi and invites them to stop by for a visit. He sends thanks to the Stamford Observatory for the chance to actually view Sirius through its telescope while writing this book.

Paul lives in Connecticut with his wife, Robin, and son, Max. *The Sirian Conspiracy* is for Max, who, like his dad, loves space and is a Wishbone fan.

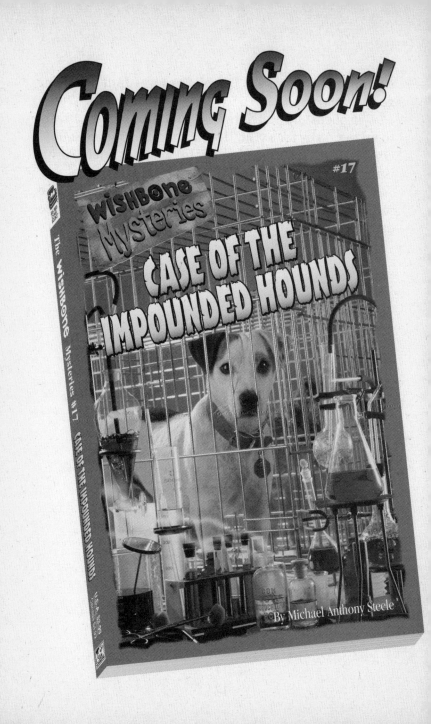

The Adventures of WISHBONE™

Read all the books in
The Adventures of Wishbone™ series!

IT'S THE DEAL OF A LIFETIME! ON THE FAN CLUB ADVENTURE OF A LIFETIME!

IT'S THE **WISHBONE™** ZONE—
THE OFFICIAL **WISHBONE FAN CLUB**!

When you enter the **WISHBONE ZONE** in 1999, you get:

- A one-year subscription to *The WISHBONE ZONE News*—that's at least four issues full of **WISHBONE** news, fun and games, and more!
- Authentic **WISHBONE** Dog Tag like the one **Wishbone™** wears! This is not for sale anywhere. Available only through this offer
- Color poster of **Wishbone**
- Exclusive suspense-filled **Adventures of Wishbone** mini-book *Tail of Terror*
- And even more great **WISHBONE** stuff!

To join the fan club, pay $10 and charge your **WISHBONE ZONE FAN CLUB** membership to VISA, MasterCard, or Discover. Call:

1-800-888-WISH

Or send us your name, address, phone number, birth date, and a check for $10 payable to Big Feats! Entertainment (TX residents add $.83 sales tax). Write to:

WISHBONE ZONE
P.O. Box 9523
Allen, TX 75013-9523

Prices and offer are subject to change. Place your order now!

©1999 Big Feats! Entertainment. All rights reserved. WISHBONE, the Wishbone portrait and WISHBONE ZONE are trademarks and service marks of Big Feats! Entertainment.